Hearts on Hold

Hearts on Hold

Hearts on Hold

W Mason Dunn

"Thou hast turned for me my mourning into dancing: thou hast put off my sackcloth, and girded me with gladness"
(Psalms 30:11).

Table of Contents

Chapter 1

The sun climbed higher, sharpening the soft morning glow. A sharp shadow from the old oak executive desk stretched across the wood-look vinyl floor Whiffs of reheated broccoli pierced from the company's breakroom, and a lingering scent of coffee evoked Daisy Whittington's need for caffeine.

Daisy Whittington raised a Grambling State University coffee mug to her mouth and took a sip. A sullen scowl swept across her face as the bitter brew found a place to settle in the middle of her mouth. Hours earlier, she'd placed a steaming cup of java on her desk and dove into work.

"Ugh!"

Time had slipped away, her focus unbroken until the impulse to sip tugged at her memory. When she finally reached for it, the chill in the cup matched her diminishing energy. Fighting the urge to expel its contents, she forced a swallow.

Daisy worked for the state of Florida when her husband, Harold, began Whittington Landscaping. When Harold died of a heart attack, their oldest son, Liam, took over as man of the house and Chief Executive Officer of Whittington Landscaping. When company funds were missing, Liam decided it was time for more family involvement. At his request, Daisy agreed to work in the office for five hours each day. Donnie, her youngest son and college thespian, agreed to help in the field with the landscaping.

They worked well together, but this day began with one mishap after the other. First, the receptionist was late, then the copier stopped working, and then one of their competitors undercut their bid for a possible commercial contract on the other side of town.

"I've done enough for a Friday," she said to herself.

She backed up a few important files, reviewed and updated her to-do list, and locked away sensitive information. Daisy stretched, standing up and glancing toward the large, framed Scripture on the wall, Philippians 4:13, her personal favorite. "I can do all things through Christ who strengthens me (KJV)."

Her small office had become a reflection of her life. A photo of Harold, taken one Sunday after church, sat on one side of her desk. Next to it, sat a professional photo of Liam and Donnie, a surprise for her birthday one year. They always brought her comfort, especially on days like today when the work pressed heavier than usual. She smiled at their images before closing her planner, where she'd made a few notes for Monday.

Daisy grabbed her coffee cup and headed to the breakroom. The pungent broccoli odor engulfed the small space like a thick fog during a morning commute. Talk about a hostile work environment. With a scowl across her face, she quickly rinsed the coffee cup and returned to her office.

After shutting down her computer, Daisy filed a few lingering papers into her desk drawer. Finally, she grabbed her purse and switched off the light before heading to Liam's office.

"That's it for me. I'm leaving," she said.

"You're leaving already?" Liam looked up from his monitor. His office, a little less personal, offered bare walls and furniture stacked with documents and business books.

Daisy pointed toward the window. "It's a beautiful day. That's one of the things I love about living in Tallahassee; we enjoy nice weather almost year-round."

"True. What's the latest on the copier?"

"Sophia and I opened every cover, and checked every feed slot, and we couldn't find anything. Not even a tiny slither of paper that would cause a jam. It's still not working. The technician should be here this afternoon. Sophia is more than capable of handling things, dear."

Liam lobbed a what-did-you-just-call-me expression in Daisy's direction. The mother-son team agreed to avoid terms of endearment in the office. Daisy wasn't very good at keeping her end of the bargain. She paused for his reprimand but was interrupted by Sophia's eager voice over the intercom.

"Mr. Whittington, your two o'clock called to reschedule. He'll be in next week."

"Thank you," said Liam, raising a fist in the air in enthusiasm. "Glad he canceled. I could use the extra hour to work on something else."

"Who were you scheduled to see?"

"Someone who wanted to discuss landscaping for his home."

"We have people to do that. Why don't you delegate the task to one of the sales team members?"

Liam tapped a few commands on his keyboard before returning his attention to Daisy. "This guy insists on speaking with me. Dad was always big on customer service, and I want to do the same."

Daisy admired her son's aspiration to continue the legacy his father built. Providing excellent customer service was at the top of the list.

No words could express the love she felt for both her sons. The moment she laid eyes on them at the adoption agency, Daisy knew God had given her double for her trouble. Years of failed attempts to conceive had not diminished her desire to be a mother. She and Harold decided to adopt. They were overjoyed when the agency notified them of two young brothers who needed a home.

"Honey," she said after a moment of reflection. "Have I told you lately that I'm proud of you?"

"Yes. Everyday." Liam stood, walked to his mother, and pulled her petite five-foot-four-inch frame into a big bear hug.

Daisy relished the overwhelming gesture of warmth and love. It was a deep connection of affection, strength, and security all at once.

"And Mom …" he said, releasing the embrace.

"Yes?"

"Watch it with the *honeys* and the *dears* in the office. We agreed, remember?"

"Okay. I'll see you later Mr. Whittington … Sir!" Daisy threw her head back and laughed.

"Ha-ha, funny! Lorraine's going to stop by the house later this evening. Something about the engagement party if that's okay."

After a rocky courtship, the couple finally accepted the fact they were made for each other. Liam asked for her hand in marriage. Lorraine longed for a traditional wedding; Liam hoped for a quick wedding. His flesh was anxious, no doubt. Both were committed to waiting for the marriage bed to consummate the marriage.

"Of course, it's okay. I'd love to see my future daughter-in-law. Did you guys decide on a pre-marital counselor?"

"We're still searching for a Christian therapist."

"I wish your father and I had something like that available for us before we got married."

"But you seemed to have done all right."

"We had our days." Daisy shrugged. "And you and Lorraine will have your bad days as well. The difference is that you two will have tools that Harold and I didn't have."

Her boys believed she and Harold enjoyed a flawless marriage. But truth be told, their marriage was far from perfect. They'd worked hard to keep it together and to keep the difficult times out of the purview of their children.

"I hope so."

"I'm sure of it," said Daisy. "Now I really need to get going. I'll see you and Lorraine tonight."

"Hold on, let me walk you out."

Daisy headed down the hallway, and Liam followed close behind. They paused at the welcome desk. Sophia worked carefully opening mail and date stamping its contents. After firing the previous receptionist for misuse of company property, Daisy and Liam searched diligently for a replacement. Upon reading Sophia's resume and career goals, they thought she would be a perfect fit.

Sophia glanced up from her tedious task. "Congratulations, Mr. Whittington."

Daisy's ears perked like a dog when it heard the crinkle of a snack bag. "Congratulations on what?"

"I'm not sure." Liam's eyes zipped from Daisy to Sophia.

"According to this, you've been nominated for Entrepreneur of the Year!" said Sophia, waving a document in his direction.

"May I see that?" asked Daisy.

"Yes, ma'am." Sophia slipped the document into Daisy's hand.

A broad smile lit across Daisy's face as she read. "Oh, honey this is wonderful!"

"Mom." Liam's eyebrows furrowed.

"Oops," she whispered, then opted for a quick embrace. "Your hard work is paying off."

"It's not a big deal. They contacted me by phone last week, but I forgot about it. And that's what we're going to do now."

Daisy whipped her head in Liam's direction. She'd been engrossed in the content of the letter. Surely, he wasn't serious.

"Dad did the hard work. I'm standing on his shoulders."

The document clearly stated the award was for the year 2024. Harold had been dead for five years. This nomination was for Liam's hard work, but it wasn't a conversation for the workplace.

"We'll finish this discussion at home," said Daisy, carefully placing the information in her purse.

The front door opened. A middle-aged man wearing a full gray beard and a technician's uniform walked through the door pulling a large black wheeled toolbox. The name John was embroidered on his shirt. Welcomed by a trio of smiles, he returned the gesture.

His eyes landed on Daisy, bounced to Liam, and back to Daisy.

Before Sophia could greet the visitor, Liam took one step forward positioning himself in front of his mother.

Daisy and Sophia gasped at Liam's obvious distaste for John's unsolicited attention.

"Good afternoon." Liam eyed the technician before offering a handshake. "You must be here to repair the copier."

"Yes," he said with a nod.

Folding his hands across his chest, Liam shifted his weight on one hip. "Where's Rodney? He usually takes care of us."

"Rodney's out today. I took his shift."

Liam's nostrils flared. He kept his eyes trained on the technician. "Sophia, would you show John to the copier."

Daisy nodded and followed Liam out the door.

"What was that all about?" asked Daisy. "Is that the way you emulate your father's customer service?"

"With all due respect, he's not a customer. We're the customer in this situation. I didn't like the way he ogled at you. I'm sure Dad would've responded the same way."

"I didn't notice"

"It was clear he was fascinated with you."

Daisy had grown accustomed to Liam's overprotective nature. Harold had been the same way.

"I appreciate your concern, but that man was harmless."

Liam opened the door of his mother's Volvo, and she entered. After settling behind the steering wheel, she fastened her seatbelt. "I've gotta run. Rosie is waiting for me."

"Drive carefully. I love you." Liam leaned in to kiss her on the cheek.

"I love you, too."

Daisy backed out of the parking lot and merged onto Capital Boulevard. The early afternoon traffic was light considering most folks had returned to work after eating lunch or running errands. Her mind shifted to Liam. Why was he concerned about men looking at her? It'd been years since she even thought about a man in that way. Harold had been her only love. And she planned to keep it that way.

***

Daisy arrived at Rosie's two-story, three-bedroom home in less than ten minutes. The two attended the same church and became friends when they both volunteered to deliver gifts to children one Christmas. When Rosie's husband traveled for work, she spent her extra time with Daisy. Sometimes, they relaxed at each other's homes. Other times, they sought adventures throughout Tallahassee. What started as an occasional girl's night out turned into a long-lasting bond.

Daisy and Rosie chatted and giggled during the entire drive to Florida Agricultural and Mechanical University, affectionately known as FAMU. Prepared to work their glutes, quads, and calves, the women meandered through the highest of seven hills. Savory aromas from the campus cafeteria and university food courts hovered in the air. Clusters of students sprinkled the well-manicured campus. The duo pressed toward the majestic white edifice fixed among the buildings housed along the quad.

"Back in the day, Donzel and I were campus sweethearts. We walked all over this campus like we didn't have a care in the world. Today, I walk from the parking lot up the hill, and my legs are on fire," said Rosie, gasping for air.

Daisy threw her head back and laughed. "Getting around the campus was much easier back then, huh?"

"Yes, it was. The distance hasn't changed but my age and weight sure have."

They walked a bit further, slowing the pace.

"We made it," said Daisy, who inhaled a calming breath before leading the way up the stairs to the museum.

They each leaned against one of the large columns on the porch of the Meek-Eaton Black Archives Research Center and Museum. The majestic two-story, white brick structure had been added to the National Register of Historic Places in 1996. Its walls shouldered diverse exhibits centered around African American history in Florida.

"I've always thought this was a beautiful stately building," said Rosie.

"Me, too. Not only the aesthetics but its solemn ambiance."

A tribute to Dr. James N. Eaton, founder, and United States Congresswoman Carrie P Meek, financial strategist, greeted them just inside the entrance. After reading the title labels, the duo began their tour, heels clanking along the hardwood floor. They spent the next hour viewing and discussing historical displays of African art and artifacts, rare papers dating back to slavery, blacks in the military, and other relics.

"This is overwhelming," said Daisy. Every moment she spent viewing the display deepened her admiration and respect for their forefathers.

"I know. I'm glad these items have been preserved. Can you imagine the things our forefathers had to endure?"

"And we have these artifacts because someone thought enough to preserve them. If they didn't stand up for justice, Whittington Landscaping probably wouldn't be here today. That's why we must give back to our community ..."

Rosie's lips curled to one side. "Don't look now, but there's a handsome man on the other side of the room watching you."

Daisy tugged at her purse strap and hiked one eyebrow, turning her head slightly.

"Don't look! He'll think we're talking about him."

Daisy snatched her head back toward Rosie. "We *are* talking about him."

"You know what I mean. Wait until he looks away." Rosie kept a straight face, like a private investigator on an episode of *Cheaters*.

"This is silly. What are we? Teenagers? He's probably a Whittington Landscaping customer."

"Now..." Rosie whispered.

"Now what?"

"Now you can look."

Daisy turned quickly for a sneak peek. Her eyes caught his and lingered for a moment. She snubbed the hurried throbbing of her heart, feeling like a schoolgirl. "No, I don't recognize him."

"That's not the point. The point is he was checking you out."

"I doubt that. Can we finish our tour, please?"

"Sure." Rosie jostled her fingers in the air and strolled to the next display.

"Just think, if we were born in a different time, I wouldn't have been allowed to own a business. Whittington Landscaping couldn't exist legally."

"Excuse me for interrupting. Did I hear you say you were a business owner?" a deep baritone voice rang out from behind them.

When the ladies turned to the sound of the voice, their eyes fell upon Daisy's alleged admirer. The man stood about six foot four inches. A short, groomed salt and pepper afro framed his face. A pair of jeans and a white buttoned-down collared shirt alluded to a nicely toned physique.

"I don't mean to pry, but I'm Ezekiel Daniel. I'm always looking to network with other black business owners." He shook their hands.

"Yeah, right!" Rosie smirked, giving him a quick once over. "Your name is Ezekiel Daniel? Like two consecutive books of the Bible?"

"Rosie!"

Trying to find a comfortable stance after Rosie's inconsiderate comment, Daisy shifted her weight from one foot to the other.

"It's fine. I get that response often." Reaching into his suit pocket, Zeke retrieved two business cards, handing one to each of the women.

Rosie read the card aloud, "Ezekiel Daniel, Real Estate Investor."

Now even more embarrassed, Daisy lobbed a hand over her heart and clenched her arm with the other. "Mr. Daniel, I apologize for my friend."

"No problem."

"Sorry about that. I thought you were joking. But since you are looking to network, this is Daisy. She's the owner of Whittington Landscaping." Rosie nodded toward her friend. "Perhaps you've heard of them?"

"Yes. Of course."

Rosie's eyes widened. "Daisy, give him one of your cards."

"What?"

Rosie glanced between Ezekiel and Daisy. Her eyes remained on Ezekiel, and a mischievous smile spread across her face. "He's interested in networking with business owners."

Daisy combed her purse for a card and handed it to Ezekiel. "This is the number to the office. Please give us a call, we'd love to chat with you. Now if you will excuse us, Mr. Daniel, it's about time for us to leave."

"Please call me Zeke. I'll give you a call next week." He looked at Daisy the way an artist gazes at a masterpiece.

"You should ask for my son, Liam." With a wave of her hand, Daisy beckoned for Rosie to follow her out the door.

"What's your problem?" asked Rosie when they reached the exit door.

"You've got to stop doing that!"

"Doing what?"

Daisy exhaled sharply. She paused at the top of the stairs. "Trying to be a matchmaker. You're not good at it."

Rosie smirked. "How do you know? Maybe I am good at it, but you'll never know because you won't take my advice."

"I've told you a million times, I'm not interested in meeting anyone. My life is fine just the way it is."

"All you do is work and take care of your sons. You hang out with me like we're dating or something. I don't know how to tell you this, but I'm happily married, and I'm breaking up with you."

The two engaged in a stare-down before Daisy relented, turned on her heels, and headed down the stairs.

"You can't break up with me."

"Why?"

Daisy chuckled. "Because I'm your ride home."

Chapter 2

Networking opportunities! Was that the best he could do?

Zeke Daniel had distanced himself from the world of dating, choosing the safety of being alone. But having seen the beautiful creature admiring the richness of their ancestry, he understood how precious the moment truly was. It was the reason he followed her, listening to her words of appreciation for each display. And when she spoke about her business, he took advantage of the open door. But networking? Seriously!

Surrounded by the beautifully crafted artifacts, stunning historical photographs, and intricate quilts and textiles. One thing stood out to Zeke. It was Daisy Whittington's beauty and understated elegance. Maybe it was the way her salt and pepper tresses framed her caramel-colored face. Perhaps it was her confident style and poise. Zeke couldn't identify what drew him to her, but it began the minute he laid eyes on her.

He'd only arrived in Tallahassee a few months earlier. Jacksonville, North Carolina, had been his home for the last ten years. The city was his last duty station before retiring from the Marine Corps. After twenty years of honorable service, he made the difficult decision to leave the military in hopes of improving his marriage. Things appeared to be getting better until his wife was killed in a terrible car accident. Everything spiraled after that. So, when one of his Marine Corps buddies contacted him with a business deal in Tallahassee, Florida, Zeke jumped on the opportunity. He and Arthur recently closed on their third commercial property. Their latest acquisition was to be converted into a quaint African American bookstore. Zeke planned to meet his partner, Arthur, at the Black Archives in search of decorative ideas and concepts.

Mesmerized, he watched as Daisy enjoyed the various displays with her friend. Before long, his attempt to remain inconspicuous failed when she turned to meet his eyes. Surely, they must have thought he was some kind of stalker. So, he concocted an excuse for staring. And it worked because he now had a name and a number.

He watched the women walk out the door, wishing he could once again inhale Daisy's flowery fragrance. It was not the first time a beautiful woman had caught his attention, and he'd let her slip away.

After losing his wife in a car accident, he vowed never to fall in love again. But there was something different about this Daisy woman. He retrieved her business card from the front pocket of his pants.

Daisy Whittington, he mused, scanning the printed information. *If I hadn't officially declared myself off the market, our initial meeting would have gone a little differently. What's your story, anyway? I didn't see a ring on your finger. You mentioned a son, where's the father?*

"Hey, Zeke." Arthur Graves, retired Marine, business mogul, and Zeke's best friend tapped him on the shoulders.

Arthur's voice snatched him out of his thoughts.

"How's it going, Arthur? Are you ready to do this?" They exchanged handshakes.

"Of course. Have you had a chance to look at either of the meeting rooms?"

"No. I was a little distracted."

"It's easy to do when you're in a space with such historical artifacts." Arthur scanned the room.

Zeke placed his hands in his pockets, jiggling his keys. "It wasn't an artifact that caught my attention."

"Okay. Who and where is she?" asked Arthur, a self-proclaimed ladies' man after two failed marriages. "For someone who has deemed himself off the market, you never miss a pretty face."

"I'm not looking for a relationship, but I can appreciate a pretty face," said Zeke. "But there's something different about Daisy …" His thoughts drifted as Daisy's image flashed across his mind.

"Daisy? You got a name this time." Arthur raised his arm in a fist pump. "Now that's progress."

"It's all about networking. She owns a Landscaping business, and I mentioned networking adventures. I thought she might be interested."

"Okay, okay!" Arthur shook his head in approval. "So, give her a call."

"And say what? I don't have an event to invite her to."

"Then, my friend," Arthur placed his arm on Zeke's shoulder. "You need to find one or create one."

Zeke thought about finding an event in the area. Networking was Arthur's area of responsibility. Zeke worked best behind the scenes with the finances. Besides, he wasn't very good at dating. Since his wife died, he'd only gone on a couple of dates. Casual dating and one-night stands weren't appealing to him.

If he found such an event and called Whittington Landscaping, would Daisy speak to him? She'd suggested that he talk to her son, Liam. And if she did speak with Zeke, would she accept his invitation? What if she insisted Liam attend the event?

"I'm sure you'll figure it out. If not, I'm here to help," said Arthur, pointing toward the stairs. "Let's view the meeting rooms. I have an appointment scheduled on the other side of town in a little over an hour."

Zeke decided to focus on the business at hand.

***

In her kitchen that evening, Daisy put the finishing touches on her charcuterie board as she listened to CeCe Winans croon "The

Goodness of God" through the Bluetooth speakers. Visions of the charming gentleman from the Black Archives with salt-and-pepper hair danced in her mind. No matter how often she tried to reconcile her thoughts, Ezekiel Daniel kept showing up like an unresolved bookkeeping error. What was it about this man?

Call her a spinster, golden girl, or pejorative old maid. Daisy believed it was impossible to experience real love twice in one lifetime. Harold and she shared something many people would never find. Even after many years of marriage, they enjoyed each other's company. If she never loved again, she'd loved enough.

Memories of Harold filled her home. His favorite armchair, where he sat to read or watch TV was still positioned in the living room. Several photographs of him were displayed throughout the house. His collection of Bible commentaries lay on the table next to his side of the bed. His home office remained virtually untouched and seldom used. And his favorite "World Greatest Dad" coffee mug stayed prominently displayed on the corner of the desk.

Life was difficult after his death. Grief propelled her into a spiraling depression. She thanked God daily for bringing her out of the darkness. Even now, five years later, grief occasionally emerged through a familiar aroma, sound, or experience. Now she understood the words her mother often said, "If it had not been for the Lord on my side, I wouldn't have made it."

Like a member of an Olympic relay team, Liam took the baton from his father and continued the race. He moved in with Daisy, ensuring she had a reason to get up each morning. He took over the business, bringing in new ideas and clients. Liam also made sure the finances were available for Donnie to complete his degree program, even though he had little interest in doing so.

Daisy lifted the charcuterie board full of cured meats, cheeses, crackers, and various fruit and nuts from the kitchen counter, gingerly transporting it to the living room. Liam and Lorraine sat together on the couch with their bodies angled toward each other. His arm was poised on the back of the sofa, his fingers gently tracing patterns on Lorraine's shoulders. He sprang from the sofa, relieving Daisy of the board as she entered the room.

"Did you and Mrs. Rosie have a good time at the museum?" he asked.

"Yes, we did. We always enjoy our time there." She returned to the kitchen for plates and utensils.

After placing the board on the coffee table, Liam returned to his position next to Lorraine. "That's something we could do together," Liam said to Lorraine. "Have you visited the Black Archives?"

"Yes, several times," she responded. "Daddy says it would be a shame not to take advantage of such a resource."

"I agree with your father," Daisy said, placing the items on the table and sitting on the loveseat. "Liam, would you bless the food so we can eat."

Liam did as his mother asked. She recalled how Harold taught their sons the importance of giving thanks and praise to God for their food. He'd done a good job preparing the boys for what would one day be their responsibility. Now that Liam had found the woman he wanted to marry, he would soon be leading the prayer in his household.

Daisy picked up the tongs and handed them to Lorraine, who mouthed, "Thank you."

"Liam said you wanted to talk to me about the engagement party. Just tell me what you want, and I'll do it."

"Aww, you're so sweet. Thank you," said Lorraine, her smile and eyes bright with appreciation. She placed a few smoked sausages, dried apricots, and artisan crackers on her plate. "Dee offered to host. She's taking care of everything. We're searching for a venue. When we narrow down the list, would you mind looking at a few of them with us? I'd love to have your opinion."

"That would be fun. Thank you for including me."

The ladies watched curiously as Liam heaped a pile of salami, chorizo, smoked sausage, and a few breadsticks on his plate.

Daisy squinted and shook her head.

He plopped a smoked sausage in his mouth and chewed rapidly. "What? You want us to eat it, right?"

They shared a laugh.

Lorraine continued. "I don't want a fancy party. I was thinking about something intimate with our close friends and family. I leave for Fort Lauderdale on Monday for business. This assignment should take about two weeks. We'll start to narrow down the choices when I return."

"Don't forget, I'm joining her for a few days next week." Liam's reminder was muffled with breadsticks.

"You are?" asked Daisy, her gaze fixed on Liam.

"Not in the same room…not even the same hotel!" hastily explained Lorraine, placing her hand on her chest. "We're committed to waiting until after the wedding to consummate the marriage."

An embarrassed chuckle escaped Daisy's lips. "No, dear, I'm not questioning the sleeping arrangements. Liam told me you recently rededicated your life to Christ. I respect you for that."

After a moment of awkward silence, Daisy turned to Liam. "It's just that today I met someone interested in networking. I advised him to call the office and ask for you. I forgot you were going out of town."

Liam nodded. "I'm sure you can handle it."

Zeke's image popped into Daisy's thoughts and butterflies tickled her stomach. The deep tone of his voice made her heart pound. The truth was Ezekiel Daniel caused her to feel something she hadn't felt in a long time. Perhaps it was the way his eyes danced or the deep throaty sound of his voice. Daisy couldn't discount the attraction, regardless of her deep-seated love for Harold and how she desperately missed him.

Chapter 3

Across town, Zeke stepped into a 2,000-square-foot smart home, a gift to himself celebrating his new start in life. His security system chimed, signaling the front door was secure. Adjusting to his arrival, the lights gradually brightened to a warm, golden hue as he entered the living room. The scent of polished wood and a slight trace of lavender from the automatic air freshener filled the room. He looked around the minimally decorated space and smiled. He loved every deliberate detail differing from what he left behind.

Reaching for his Mac laptop on the coffee table, Zeke settled on his black leather sofa. It was the first time he'd lived more than fifty miles away from a military base. After entering a few commands, an electronic copy of The Marine Corps Times appeared on the screen. He needed to research updates or changes to his military benefits.

As much as he tried, he couldn't concentrate. Daisy Whittington's image filled every unoccupied space in his head. Soon, she was all he could think about. But why? He wasn't in search of female companionship. His life was finally flowing in the right direction. He'd sold the old house and all its memories. Marriage had not been kind to him, and he didn't want anything to do with the institution or anything that would lead him in its direction.

Zeke removed his ringing iPhone from the table. His daughter's image lit up the screen. Esther called every day and hers was the one female voice he looked forward to hearing. She was a kind, loving daughter with many of the characteristics of her biblical namesake.

"Hey, Baby Girl."

"Hey, Dad. How are you?" Those were always her first words when she called. Esther worried about her father. She fought against his decision to move to Tallahassee, believing he was running away from the memories of her mother. But Zeke disagreed. He wasn't running away from anything. Instead, he was moving forward to the next chapter of his life. A chapter that didn't include memories of his dead wife or the nightmare she created before leaving this world.

"I'm fine. Just getting home. How's everyone there?"

"Great. Did you make any new friends today?" she teased.

"Not again. Honey, I told you I'm not lonely."

"Dad, even the Bible says it's not good for man to be alone. You need a help meet."

Familiar with the verse from Genesis, Zeke laughed. Back home, women were eager to fill the void they imagined he carried. Friends and relatives repeatedly introduced him to single women. After-church invitations for a home-cooked meal were a frequent thing when he lived in Jacksonville, but none of them appealed to him. That's when he decided the best thing to do was to move away from the place that held his story.

"Honey don't worry. I'm not lonely. There's plenty to keep me busy. I'm looking over information about military benefits. Then I'll review the financials from today, and I'll close out the evening with one of my Madden video games. It doesn't get any better than that," he said, trying to convince not only his daughter but himself.

"Okay, Dad. I'll let you go. Besides, I need to get dinner started. Garland took Elsa to the park, and they'll be back soon."

"Okay. Glad to hear Garland is keeping up with his daddy duties."

After saying goodbye, Zeke returned his attention to the Marine Corps Times. He absentmindedly read through the articles, then searched the internet for an electronic copy of the local newspaper, *Tallahassee Democrat*. His eyes fell upon an article about an event he'd attended with Arthur the previous month. Working Class Wednesday was a monthly event that brought businesses and the community together. It was scheduled to convene again on the upcoming Wednesday. Daisy's image fell across his mind. He recalled her warm brown eyes and kind smile. Soft curly hair framed her oval-shaped, sweet face. He was overcome by the vivid clarity with which he remembered her.

I should invite her to attend, but she made it clear that her son was the one who participated in networking activities. I'm going to need to convince her to go with me. Maybe I'll call the office on Monday morning. That won't work. If I call the office, she'll just transfer me to her son. Perhaps an in-person visit will do the trick. I'll give it my best shot.

Chapter 4

On Monday, the office was alive with motion by mid-morning. Phones rang in tandem as Sophia juggled incoming client calls. Designers huddled in the conference room, debating plant placements and irrigation layouts. Daisy's keyboard clicked as she updated payroll, her fingers moving in sync with the hum of the printer churning out contracts and invoices. Crew members fresh off the job buzzed through the doors, their boots tracking a bit of dirt across the floor. Daisy wished she had another pair of hands. With Liam out of town, responsibility for ongoing office operations fell on her.

Gentle sounds of John P. Kee singing, "I Do Worship," played softly in the background. Daisy considered the lyrics to be but comforting.

"Are you holding up okay," asked Sophia, walking in with a stack of documents.

Daisy looked up from the computer screen. "Yes, I am. Have you heard from Joe Walton? I'm waiting for him to submit time for his section."

"No. I haven't." Sophia placed a couple of documents on the desk for his signature. "That's the third time in a row that he's missed the deadline. I'll reach out to him."

"Thank you." Daisy sat up straight and pursed her lips. "I know that he's new to the foreman position, but I need to come up with a way to convey the importance of submitting documents on time."

"I'll get right on it." Sophia grabbed a few papers from the outgoing box and walked out the door.

I bet he'd remember to submit them in a timely fashion if I forgot his paycheck. Forgive me, Lord, but Joe is holding up progress. I need to finish the payroll and check on the inventory list before leaving this afternoon.

Daisy glanced at the various papers lining the top of her desk. Whittington Landscaping was growing by leaps and bounds. There was a time when Harold spent most of his day drumming up business. These days, not only did they have a plethora of repeat customers, but they were gaining new customers daily. God had been faithful to them and, for that, she was grateful.

Sophia's voice ringing over the intercom ended her musing. "Mrs. Whittington, there's a Zeke Daniel on the line for you."

Daisy stared at the phone and her fingers roamed along her collarbone. She sucked her bottom lip and froze for several seconds.

"Mrs. Whittington are you there?" asked Sophia.

"Yes, I'm here. Please transfer the call. Thank you."

"Yes, ma'am."

Daisy took a deep breath before placing the phone to her ear. "Hello, Mr. Daniel."

"Good morning. Please call me Zeke. It was a pleasure meeting you last week. Did you enjoy your visit to the museum?"

Daisy glanced at the payroll data on her computer screen. There was work to be done, and she didn't have time for chitchat. But something was soothing about the sound of Zeke's voice. Besides, it was nice to have a conversation with a male other than one of her offspring.

"I always enjoy my visits to the museum. We're blessed to have such a wonderful resource in Tallahassee, don't you think?"

"I couldn't agree with you more."

He was quiet for a few moments and she eyeballed the phone to make sure they hadn't lost the connection. "Mr. Daniel … I mean, Zeke. Are you there?"

"Yes, I'm here."

"I'm sure you didn't call to see if I enjoyed my visit to the Archives?"

"Actually, I did. But I also wanted to … Are you familiar with Working Class Wednesday?"

"Isn't that the monthly gathering of the local community and small businesses around the Big Bend?"

"Yes. It's the brainchild of one of our young black civic leaders, Terrance L. Barber. It has exploded since its inception in 2016."

"I know you mentioned something about networking when we met at the museum. My son handles those things. Unfortunately, he's out of town and won't return until the end of the week. Perhaps you can call him and schedule a time for the two of you to meet."

"Actually, I-I," Zeke stuttered. "I wanted to know if *you* would join me, not as a participant. We could enjoy the event as spectators."

Daisy sat up straight and air trapped in her throat. Had Zeke asked her to join him? She couldn't decide how to respond. So, she didn't.

Is this personal or business? I hope he knows this is business because I have no intentions of getting involved in anything personal with him or any man.

"It's going to be at Cascades Park this Wednesday… out in the open with lots of people around. Just in case you think I'm an axe murderer or something like that," he teased.

A faint giggle escaped her tightly pressed lips. Her nose wrinkled as she tried to resist the urge to laugh. "Zeke," she said, shifting in place. "I'm not accusing you of ill intent. To be honest, I've been a widow for several years. God blessed me with a wonderful husband. I'm content with my life the way it is right now," she added in a murmur as if she was attempting to convince herself.

"I understand. I lost my wife a few years ago. It's difficult to start over. If you agree to attend Working Class Wednesday

24

with me, I'll be a perfect gentleman. We'll walk around, meet a few people, and support a few local small businesses. I promise you'll enjoy yourself."

Daisy could almost see his thoughtful eyes looking back at her. They had deceased spouses in common, but it wasn't the time to dwell on it. She knew the importance of supporting small businesses. It was the support from the local community that catapulted Whittington Landscaping into the thriving business it enjoys today. How could she turn down an opportunity to reciprocate? It was good business.

She paused and then murmured, "Okay. I'll join you. Just tell me the time and place. I'll meet you there."

"How about we meet in front of the Edison Restaurant at 6:30?"

"That sounds good. Enjoy the rest of your day." She ended the call.

Daisy leaned back into her chair like a scared turtle receding into its shell. She shrank back, second-guessing the decision to accept Zeke's invitation.

Chapter 5

Fluffy bubbles swirled around the large garden tub as Daisy sank into the warm water. Lifting her chin, she inhaled the whiffs of lavender that filled the spacious bathroom. Soft calming music floated from nearby speakers and lavender-scented candles intermittently flickered in the distance. Who needs a day at the spa when a calm reset awaits at home?

The weight of the day melted as Daisy immersed her body in the soothing water. Clutters of thoughts and stresses slowly disappeared with the rising steam from the tub —customer challenges and muffling thoughts of billing and invoicing problems. Every muscle in her petite body eased as if it had been tranquilized.

Daisy hadn't realized how tense she'd been. It seemed as if glitches and hiccups happened most often when Liam was away from the office. In the three days he'd been gone, a disagreement broke out among the crew members. Without Liam to mediate, Daisy stepped in, even though she was not used to handling field issues. The computer system crashed, forcing her to manually track appointments and client requests, adding layers of stress to an already hectic day. And finally, a shipment of plants was delayed, causing backlogs and customer complaints.

Then there was Zeke. Why did the very thought of him wreak havoc on her emotions? He was just a man who'd invited her to a networking event. Their plan to meet at Cascades Park was not a date. It was a networking opportunity.

Daisy wasn't a dating expert. She'd dismissed the possibility of seeing someone. It was fine for her sons and friends, but not for her.

After the bath, she changed into a cool summer dress. The bright yellow color was complimented by eye-catching statement jewelry. Daisy checked her appearance in the full-length mirror in her bedroom. *This is not a date,* she reminded herself. Even so, she couldn't help the smile that graced her lips. She twirled for effect.

Not bad for a fifty-one-year-old.

With Liam out of town, there was no one to ask where she was going and when she would return. Although they extended such curiosity to each other for safety reasons, she looked forward to leaving the house without an interrogation. Slipping into a pair of sandals, Daisy grabbed her purse from the hall closet and headed for the door. That's when she heard the hum of the garage door opening. Donnie's Toyota Highlander appeared and pulled into the space next to her car.

She waited for him to exit before speaking. "Hi, son. It's good to see you."

"Hi, Mom. Are you headed out? Did you forget I was coming over," he asked, eyeing his mother suspiciously.

"I'm going to Cascades Park for a networking event. But I'll be back soon. I told both you and your brother that I didn't need a babysitter. There's no need to spend the night with me when he's away."

Donnie shook his head. "I'm not babysitting. Want some company?"

"Actually, I'm meeting a friend."

"Mrs. Rosie?" he asked.

She refused to look at him. "I should be back in an hour or so," she said, avoiding his question. "Make yourself at home."

Without further explanation, Daisy walked to her car, slid behind the wheel, and backed out of the driveway. When she looked at him, Donnie stood at the front door with his hands folded in front of his chest. She hadn't fooled him. She didn't want to answer questions, and he knew it.

Harold would be proud of how her boys watched over her. It was something he'd taught them from the beginning. "Show your mother that she can rely on you …Treat her with kindness and respect … Show her appreciation … Make her feel valued and loved." It was as if she could hear his voice.

Daisy drove through the neighborhood, waving at friends along the way. Turning onto Thomasville Road, the two-lane thoroughfare leading to downtown Tallahassee, she wondered what Rosie would think of her evening rendezvous.

"Hey, Siri, call Rosie." She commanded the phone system.

"Hello?"

"Hey, girl. Don't take this the wrong way, but since you broke up with me, I decided to go out without you," said Daisy with a grin.

"I don't believe it. Where are you headed?" Rosie responded, then paused.

"I'm headed to Working Class Wednesday at Cascades Park."

"That's great. But I know you're not alone. Who's going with you? Liam or Donnie?" asked Rosie, a bit of sarcasm in her tone.

"Neither. I'm meeting Mr. Ezekiel Daniel!" Daisy imagined the look of shock on Rosie's face. Mouth wide open and eyebrows shot up in disbelief. She could barely contain her amusement.

"The cutie from the museum? Are you kidding me?" Rosie chuckled. A lot, not a little.

"What's so funny?"

"Oh, please. You? On a date? Okay And I'm Tina Turner." Sarcasm dripped from every word.

"It's not a date. We're just two entrepreneurs attending a business function. It's good for Whittington Landscaping to network with the community."

Rosie chuckled. "How did this happen? I thought Liam was the one who handles networking events."

"He does. Liam is out of town, and the man called the office."

"Okay. Did he hold a gun to your head?" her voice spiked with cynicism.

"No. He did not. I don't know how he convinced me to attend. But I'm in the car and headed there now."

"What did Liam and Donnie have to say about it?"

"Nothing. I didn't tell them. Besides, it's business."

"Sure!" said Rosie. "Have fun, and I want to hear all about it afterward."

"There'll be nothing to share. We're networking, not dating."

If that's true, why do I feel like I'm betraying Harold? I should put this car in reverse, head back home, and enjoy the evening with Donnie. But that would open the door to more inquiries. Besides, Harold would never cancel a business appointment unless it was an emergency. I should keep my word. I'll meet Zeke and walk around for a little while. Then I'll make an excuse and leave. Liam will handle any further meetings between Zeke Daniel and Whittington.

"Either way, I want to hear all about it," Rosie's voice drew Daisy from her thoughts.

"I'll give you a call when I get home. Gotta go, pulling into the parking lot now."

"Have fun. Talk to you later."

Daisy disconnected the call. With a made-up mind, she found an available parking spot and walked toward the entrance of the Edison Restaurant. The building was once the city's electric and light plant in the 1920s. She spotted Zeke standing near the entrance of the beautifully restored edifice that was now one of the premier restaurants in Tallahassee. He gazed at her with admiration in his eyes. Appreciation from members of the opposite sex wasn't a foreign concept to her. She usually brushed them off and moved on. But this was different. Zeke looked at her as if she were a masterpiece, a rare piece of art. His approving eyes stirred her heart.

"Hi, there. You look beautiful," he said taking her in breathlessly.

"Thank you." She blushed. His words were so full of passion they left her speechless. The man gave new meaning to charming and debonair. He oozed confidence. "You look nice as well."

He lifted an eyebrow. "Thank you. Are you ready to check out the scene?"

She accidently inhaled in a deep whiff of his cologne, and the scent sent her heart into an erratic rhythm. The reaction surprised her. She needed to pull herself together. This networking thing had her as jumpy as a sprinkler on the fritz.

Daisy compelled herself to stop thinking about how anxious she was. She mumbled a yes.

"Great. The vendors are on the lower level, and there's music and food also. Unless you'd prefer to have a quiet dinner inside the restaurant."

"Hmm. The old bait-and-switch. That tactic is as old as the City of Tallahassee," she teased, and a grin rested at the corner of her mouth.

"No tricks here." He threw his hands in the air as if to surrender. "Just thought I'd offer. Some of my favorite food vendors are here. There's Leola's Crab Shack, Smackin' Good Wings, and several others. What's your pleasure?"

A smile swayed his lips. She had a hunch whatever he had planned was going to be fun.

"Actually, I'd like to check out the goods and services first."

"As you wish." Zeke waved a hand to move them forward.

Soon, they descended the stairs leading to a dynamic outdoor space transformed into a hotbed of activity, showcasing well-known brands. Canopies and stalls strategically positioned along the sidewalk created a seamless networking and engagement environment. Just beyond this area, an energetic outdoor food market buzzed with a diverse array of culinary delights.

Zeke and Daisy visited vendor after vendor, chatting with each one, purchasing from a few, listening to their stories, and giving advice when asked. Before she knew it, Daisy had a bag full of local products, and a wallet full of business cards. Glancing at her watch, Daisy was surprised an hour had come and gone so quickly.

"I'm sure you've worked up an appetite after all the mingling. Are you ready to check out the food vendors?" asked Zeke.

She threw up her hands. "I grabbed something to eat before I left the house. But I'd love something to drink."

"And what would the lady like to drink?" Zeke's face crinkled around his eyes into a smile.

She shrugged. "A lemonade would be great."

They walked to one of the food vendors, making small talk along the way. Daisy was surprised at how comfortable she felt with him. She watched as he purchased two lemonades and then returned to her side.

Zeke angled his head, narrowing his gaze. "Where would you like to sit?"

"How about over there?" Daisy pointed to an unoccupied bench a few feet away.

Zeke tossed a glance and a trace of a smile. "Are you having a good time?"

"I am. It's nice to see so many young entrepreneurs. Do you attend every Wednesday?" Daisy settled onto the bench. She relaxed and enjoyed the atmosphere.

"I try to attend as often as possible."

"So why did you invite me? You could have drummed out more business for yourself had you participated instead of spectating tonight."

He leaned back on the bench and smoothed a palm over his face. "The truth is I felt drawn to you."

The man is charming.

"So, I was right." She chuckled. "This whole networking thing was really a ruse?"

He practically choked on his lemonade, "Not exactly."

"Either it was or it wasn't." She challenged him.

"When I saw you, I wanted to get to know you. I don't play games with women. I know what it feels like to be hurt. Besides, tomorrow is not promised to any man. All I have is today. And I want to use this time to get to know more about you, Daisy Whittington."

She watched him curiously.

"You look like you want to ask me something," he said as if reading her mind.

"Go ahead. I'm an open book."

Daisy took a sip of lemonade before speaking. "You mentioned you were a widower. How long ago did your wife die?"

"Three years ago. Linda was killed by a drunk driver."

Daisy gasped. "I'm so sorry."

"Thank you. I have my good and bad days. It was the grace of God that kept me from losing my mind." He looked away.

"I know what you mean. When Harold died, I fell into a deep depression. We had plans. I couldn't see my life without him. Even though I had a thriving business and two wonderful sons, I couldn't see past my sorrow. But I believed then and I believe now that God will never leave or forsake me. I'm never alone."

"I share those feelings and your faith in God. Even when I'm at my lowest, He is there. People who haven't experienced the loss of a spouse can't fully understand the grief."

"That's true. They mean well. But they just can't understand."

"It's nice to talk to someone who does." Zeke's eyes met hers. Then he reached for her hand, his movements calm and intentional.

Daisy looked down at his fingers now lightly wrapped around her hand.

A silence fell between them. His tender touch conveyed support and compassion.

Suddenly, doubt surfaced like a storm cloud rolling in without warning.

Why am I letting this man hold my hand?

This is nice. His hand is soft and strong, caring, and thoughtful.

I should pull away.

But I don't want to. I kinda like it.

She smiled and gently squeezed his hand as a spark of hope and excitement found its way to her heart.

"Mrs. Whittington?" A voice rang from behind the park bench. Daisy dropped Zeke's hand like a hot baked potato. She whipped her head around to see a majestic and imposing German Shepherd sniffing the grassy area a few yards away. Standing on the sidewalk, attached to the other end of the leash was Gloria Jean Mitchell, one of her church members.

Daisy's eyes widened, and her eyebrows raised. She sprang from the bench like a Jack-in-the-box. She did a rapid about-face and muttered, "Gloria Jean, how nice to see you."

Emitting a low warning growl, the dog stood tall and alert, his gaze focused on Daisy.

"I thought that was you. But …" the young woman's probing eyes danced from Daisy to Zeke and back to Daisy.

"Oh, this is Ezekiel Daniel," she pointed a shaky finger at her companion.

Zeke stood. The German Shepard positioned himself in front of his owner and growled aggressively.

"Echo, hush!" Gloria Jean snapped her fingers and commanded the animal in a gentle tone. He obeyed.

"Zeke, this is Gloria Jean Mitchell," she said, explaining their connection. "She and her parents have been attending my church for as long as I can remember."

"Nice to meet you, ma'am. I'd shake your hand, but I don't think your pet would appreciate it."

"I understand. We get that a lot." Gloria Jean smiled, sending Daisy a curious glance.

Daisy's thoughts drifted back to those Sunday after church when Gloria Jean and her parents would visit. While Gloria Jean ran off with the boys, Daisy and Harold sat with her parents, happiness permeating the house like the aroma of warm cornbread. Those moments were pure, certain.

But now, Gloria Jean saw her on a park bench, her fingers laced with a man who wasn't Harold. A jolt of shock, a flush of embarrassment crept up her spine. Had she stepped over a line she never thought she would cross?

"Mr. Daniel is a local businessman. We're attending the Working Class Wednesday event. We took a break from the excitement, but I think it's time for me to go home," Daisy explained, nervously.

"I should get going, too," Gloria said. "One more lap around the park should tire Echo out for the evening." She turned, pulled a treat from her pocket, and offered it to her dog. Then the two headed away.

Daisy peeped at her watch before glancing at Zeke. "I should get going."

"Do you need to leave so soon?" His eyes searched hers.

"Yes, I've been here longer than I planned."

"Okay, then. I'll walk you to your car."

Daisy took a deep breath and released it. "Thanks, but I'll grab this pedicab," she said, pointing to a three-wheeled bike, hauling behind it a passenger cab. She hailed for the driver.

"I hope you had a good time," Zeke said.

"I did. Thank you for the invitation. And thank you for the lemonade."

"You're welcome. Would you like me to trash the cup?"

"Yes, thank you." She handed the cup to Zeke, who placed it next to his on the vacated bench.

The pedicab approached, and Zeke helped her inside. He pulled a five-dollar bill from his pocket and handed it to the driver before Daisy could protest. "She's parked in front of The Edison. Please take her to her car."

"Thank you," she murmured. "I'll give your number to Liam when he returns."

***

Zeke wasn't fooled. He saw how she struggled to maintain eye contact. The tone of her voice shifted from joyful to anxious. Gloria's presence had badly shaken Daisy. He speculated about the history between them.

The red two-seater pedicab inched toward The Edison parking lot. Refusing to look away, Zeke watched until the vehicle reached its intended destination. He may not have understood Daisy's actions, but he wanted to ensure she made it safely to her vehicle.

I thought we were beginning to connect. She shared her feelings of grief, and I felt safe enough to do the same. Things only a person who'd lost a spouse would understand. She even allowed me to hold her hand...

Zeke watched closely as the driver disembarked the vehicle to assist Daisy with her exit. She entered her car and pulled out of the parking lot without looking back.

Zeke returned to the park bench. Everything had been fine until Gloria Jean appeared with her Amazon guard dog. Sadly, he understood Daisy's dilemma. The first time he was out in public with another woman after his wife's death was awkward as well. He was past the guilt of it all. But Daisy wasn't. She needed time.

Zeke stood, tossed both cups in the trash, and headed for his vehicle.

***

The setting sun cast a warm, golden light bathing the Killearn subdivision as Daisy made her way home. Golden lights painted the sky in hues of orange and pink. Her home stood hidden among the tall trees of the premier golf course community. The house was built in 1975. Daisy and her husband purchased it in 1985. She recalled how Harold labored to turn the bare parcel of land into the beautifully landscaped property it was today.

Donnie's car was still in the garage when she arrived. Even though she protested his decision to spend the night, deep down she appreciated his gesture. Acts of service was one of her love languages.

After entering the house, Daisy rested her purse on the kitchen table. She glanced into the living room at Donnie sitting on the sofa watching television. He stood and walked toward her.

"Did you and Mrs. Rosie have a good time?"

Daisy shook her head. "I never said I was with Mrs. Rosie. But I had a good time. Have you eaten?"

Donnie placed a tender kiss on her forehead. "I had a ham and cheese sandwich. But I could eat another one."

"Great," said Daisy. "I'll get the meat, cheese, and bread. You get the lettuce and tomato."

Daisy washed her hands at the kitchen sink. She enjoyed preparing meals for her sons, but she also requested their assistance in the kitchen on occasion. She'd taught them how to cook and clean. Harold and she believed they weren't just raising boys to be men; they were raising husbands and fathers.

After removing two small plates from the counter, Daisy filled each of them with two slices of bread. "How are your classes coming along? Are you getting excited about graduation?"

"Yes, ma'am." Donnie washed his hands and retrieved a tomato from the refrigerator. Then he took a knife from a nearby drawer. "You were gone for almost two hours. I was beginning to worry about you."

"No need to worry. I was fine," Daisy said in a kind tone. "I know how to take care of myself."

"I know you can," she observed a range of emotions race over his face before he continued. "We worry because we've already lost one parent." He paused, shaking his head. "We don't want to lose another." His eyes begged for understanding.

Donnie's words hit a familiar nerve. She turned to place a hand on her son's shoulder. "I know what it feels like to lose a parent. Both my parents have transitioned. It's painful and scary. But we can't change it. All we have is each other now. We can spend our time worrying about losing each other or we can spend the time enjoying each other."

He sighed. "I know, Mom. But—"

She raised a hand to stop him. "I don't want you or your brother to place me on a pedestal. I'm a human being just like the two of you. God doesn't want you to love anyone or anything more than you love Him. And one day, I will leave this world. But your Heavenly Father will always be there for you."

Donnie nodded in agreement.

After arranging the ingredients onto the bread, Daisy placed the sandwiches on the table.

"Tea or water?" he asked.

"Water for me."

Donnie filled two glasses with the beverages and joined his mother at the table. He blessed the food and took a bite in one continuous motion.

"Some things never change." Daisy teased. "You've had a ferocious appetite since the day we brought you home."

He frowned. "I can't help myself."

Donnie updated his mother on his degree progression as they enjoyed their sandwiches. When they finished eating, he began clearing the table. "You never answered my question. Who did you meet at the park tonight?"

Before she could respond, Daisy's phone pinged.

"Hey, Rosie," she answered.

"I tried to wait for your call, but you were taking too long. Tell me everything!" her friend ordered.

"There were a lot of vendors," said Daisy, glancing at Donnie to see if he was eavesdropping.

"I'll take care of the cleanup. You chat with Mrs. Rosie."

"Thanks. Now stop listening to my conversation," she fussed, moving down the hall to her bedroom.

"He's just checking up on his mother," said Rosie.

"It appears you are as well."

"Yes, I am. So, what happened?"

"Nothing really," Daisy entered her bedroom, closed the door, and settled onto the bed bench. "He's a nice man. A conversationalist. Did I mention he was widowed?"

"No, you didn't."

"After visiting the vendors, we found a bench and talked a little bit about what life is like without our spouses," said Daisy, choosing not to include the information about holding his hand.

"Are you going to see him again?"

"If he's looking for landscaping services, then yes. Other than that, I can't think of a reason to see him again."

"Companionship!"

"I enjoyed spending time with him tonight. It was great. But I'm not looking for companionship. I'm not interested in investing my time or energy."

"Maybe meeting the right person will change your mind."

"Not gonna happen. Listen, it's been a long night. I need some rest."

"Okay, then. We'll talk tomorrow."

Daisy disconnected the call and exhaled, willing herself to shake off the heaviness pushing on her chest. It was just networking. Just a conversation. But when she glanced at the framed picture on her nightstand—Harold's easy smile suspended in time—the logic unraveled. Her stomach tightened. Had she just devoted the evening laughing with another man? She looked away, but guilt had already taken over, thick and unwavering.

Chapter 6

Thursday morning, Daisy stepped out of her car. She couldn't help but smile. The soft glow of the morning sun stretched lazily across the city bathing the earth in a warm golden light. She closed her eyes for a moment, letting the cool, crisp air wrap around her like an old friend. A gentle breeze rolled in the fragrance of blooming flowers. It was a simple pleasure, but she'd learned that life was made up of moments like these.

Her mind wandered to the previous night's *nondate* with Zeke. His deep voice still lingered in her thoughts. It had been an almost perfect night until she let fear take over. If she never heard from Zeke again, it would be her fault.

Determined to keep her mind off Zeke and on the work at hand, Daisy walked into the building, greeted Sophia, and began reconciling inventory. A call from an irritated crew leader haltered her progress. She knew something was off when Sophia announced that Alan Davis was on the line. A call from him usually meant a manpower shortage or injury.

"Morning, ma'am," Alan spoke with urgency.

"Morning, Alan. Is everything all right?"

"John Coates called in sick, and we're short one man. We could use an extra hand."

Daisy's fingers danced across the keyboard and the field management software appeared on her screen. With a few additional keystrokes, Alan's crew was fully manned, and she continued working on inventory. Progress was once again short-lived. Sophia transferred another call.

"This is Daisy."

"Good morning, Daisy. This is Zeke."

Unable to move, she sat in utter disbelief he'd called. Simultaneously, her mind drifted to their last meeting. The comfort they felt toward each other was understandable. They were both grieving the death of a spouse. Yet, Daisy couldn't bring herself to regret the time she'd spent in the park with Zeke.

With mixed emotions, she hesitated. She was happy to hear his voice, but a bit embarrassed about how the prior night ended. "Hello," she murmured.

"I wanted to make sure you're okay. I would've called last night, but I didn't have your cell number."

Leaning back in her chair, she smiled. "Yes, I made it home safely. Thanks for checking. I'm glad you called because I wanted to apologize for leaving abruptly."

"No apology necessary. I get it. You felt guilty being in public with another man. And you probably felt worse when your friend showed up."

"That's exactly what happened."

"A year after my wife died, I invited a woman to church. She sat next to me during the service. It felt like everyone in the sanctuary was giving me the side-eye. Guilt stricken, I visited other churches for a while. A few weeks later, my pastor called to check on me. He pried the truth out of me and made me realize what I was feeling was normal."

"Thanks for sharing that." Daisy covered the phone with her hand and released a deep sigh. "Do you date often?"

"No. Not very often. But for some reason, I'd like to know more about you."

The last thing she needed was for Zeke to know how attracted she was to him. Although, she supposed he already knew. "I'm not that interesting."

"Would you mind if I called you on your cell some other time when you're not working?"

She hesitated. *If I give him my number, will I be sending mixed messages? I don't think so because I've already told him that I'm not looking for a relationship. Besides, neither is he. It'd be nice to talk with someone who understands what I'm going through. What harm would it do to have a few conversations with him?*

"I think I'd like that."

"What would be a good time to call?"

A smile stirred her lips. "In the evening before nine."

"Of course."

She recited her cell number and excused herself from the call. Before she could start the next task, Sophia rang in again.

"Liam's on the line."

"Thanks."

"Good morning, son. Shouldn't you be spending time with your fiancé?"

"She's working. So am I. How are you doing, Mom?"

Daisy leaned back in her chair. She wanted to tell him to hurry back to the office because she needed his assistance. But there was no way she could let him know things were overwhelming. "I'm fine. John Coates called in sick this morning. The crew leader said they needed an extra man, so I made some staffing adjustments and got someone else out there."

"John has a habit of calling in at the last minute. That creates a shortage of manpower and can often put others at risk. I'll address that when I return. Thanks for handling it."

"Maybe we should reconsider the way we calculate workforce capacity."

"You're probably right. Some of our competitors have experienced high turnover costs due to shortages in manpower and burnout. We've been successful because we remain fully staffed and our guys aren't overworked. Sooner or later, we're going to have to add staff to the crews. Good idea, Mom. Would you like to work with me on this?"

Daisy shook her head as if Liam could see her.

As the company's Chief Executive Officer, Liam kept his mother and brother informed on all aspects of the business. He'd done well using his MBA to not only sustain but also to grow the business. Harold recognized Liam's business acuity long before he'd set foot onto a college campus. It was what Liam loved to do, and he was good at it.

"I'd have to give it some thought. Remember, I came out of retirement to be in the office a few hours each day. I have no aspirations of working full time."

"Understood. I'll meet with the foreman when I return. His input is vital."

"I'll have Sophia make the arrangements."

"Thanks. And Mom, you're doing a great job. Please don't try to handle everything by yourself. Sophia is there to assist. So are the foreman and crew leaders."

After disconnecting the call, Daisy walked to the window thinking about her son.

Liam is brilliant. He's worked hard to make Whittington Landscaping successful. Harold would be proud of him. If anyone deserves to be nominated for Entrepreneur of the Year, it's Liam. Why is he fighting against it? Harold would agree. One way or another, I'll get him to see that.

Harold's absence changed our lives. Both Liam and Donnie are adjusting to life without their father. And so am I. It's not easy to just move on. But I am looking forward to chatting with Zeke on the phone. Maybe we can get to know each other out of the eyes of the public. It could be our little secret.

***

At the end of the day, Daisy jumped into the Volvo and proceeded to Governor's Square Mall. The engagement party was a week away and nothing in her current wardrobe would suffice for the event. Two hours later, she returned home with three dresses, a blouse, and three pairs of shoes. Each new piece was mixed and matched with a current item in her closet. She examined each outfit in the mirror and tucked the combination in her mind for later use. Then came the arduous task of storing everything in its rightful place. Her phone rang, and she answered it, grateful for the distraction.

"Hello."

"Hi, Daisy. This is Zeke. Did I catch you at a bad time?"

"No, I was just putting away a few things I purchased at the mall. How are you?"

"I'm fine. Thank you for sharing your number with me."

Her heart fluttered at the sound of his voice. It was nice to chat without worry of being seen.

"I'm glad you called." Daisy crossed the room and sat in the Queen Anne chair.

"Did you find anything good at the mall?"

She pulled her knees up and encircled them with one arm. "I was searching for a dress for my son's engagement party. However, I found a few other things as well."

"Liam, right?"

He remembered. How thoughtful.

Her heart warmed toward him.

"Yes, he's my oldest. I have two sons, Liam and Donnie. What about you? Do you have children?"

"I have one daughter, Esther. She's married with one child. They live in North Carolina."

Daisy frowned. She couldn't imagine living two states away from her children. Liam and Donnie were grown men, who had lives of their own. So did she. But they were a constant part of each other's lives, and she wanted to keep it that way.

"What prompted you to move to Tallahassee?"

"Memories. Jacksonville, North Carolina, was my last duty station in the Marine Corps. The year before I retired, my wife and I bought a house. Shortly after that, she was killed in a car accident, and everything began to unravel. I needed a change. An old Marine Corps buddy of mine lives here. He reached out to me about a real estate deal and asked if I would consider becoming his business partner. Esther was happily married and doing well. I accepted his offer, and here I am. I was reluctant to move at first, but I needed a change. And Tallahassee offered a chance to start anew. So, I took it."

"I'm sorry you went through that. Do the memories still haunt you when you visit Esther?"

"My daughter lives in Wilmington, about an hour away from Jacksonville and the Marine Corps Base Camp Lejeune. I can visit her without stepping foot in Jacksonville."

"How has she dealt with your wife's death?"

"Not so good at first. She was close to her mother. My unit deployed often. It was just the two of them at home most of the time. After my wife died, Esther cried a lot. I didn't know how to handle her tears. It's only by the grace of God we made it through. A lot of people like to use that phrase arbitrarily, but I mean it. I don't deserve the relationship I now share with my daughter. God used a situation that could have torn us apart to bring us closer. All things work together …"

"… for good to them that love God, to them who are the called according to *his* purpose," she recited along with him.

Daisy smiled. "Romans 8 verse 28, one of my favorite Bible verses."

"How have your sons dealt with their father's death?"

"We all had a hard time in the beginning. People seem to think Christians are exempt from difficult times. But I was saved and sad. My boys came together, covered me with their prayers, and made sure I had what I needed."

"Sounds like they're protective of their mother."

"That's an understatement. Liam moved in with me, and Donnie may as well have done the same. He's over here just about every day. In fact, when Liam's out of town, Donnie spends the night."

They were still chatting an hour later when Donnie knocked on her bedroom door.

"I'll be out in a few minutes," she said, covering the phone with her hand.

"Is everything okay?" asked Zeke.

"Yes. That was Donnie. I should get off the phone and greet him. Can you believe we've been talking for over an hour?" she asked, glimpsing at her watch.

"May I ask a question before we say good night?"

Daisy gnawed on her lower lip, speculating about the forthcoming inquiry. "Sure."

"There's a bowl-a-thon next weekend to raise money for sickle cell disease. Would you like to join me? Should be a great time, and it's for a great cause."

Daisy thought about how her second cousin, Lisa, was diagnosed with Sickle Cell Anemia shortly after birth. She was constantly in the hospital. Eventually, Lisa underwent a successful bone marrow transplant. Daisy welcomed the opportunity to raise awareness of the disease.

"Just tell me when and where."

"Next Friday night. Capital Lanes on Capital Circle Northeast. I'd be happy to pick you up."

Suddenly, an image of Liam and Donnie standing at the front door with weapons crossed her mind.

"No, thank you. That won't be necessary. I'll meet you there."

"I've enjoyed speaking with you. May I call you tomorrow?"

The impulse to deny his request lingered, but Daisy resisted. Another opportunity to chat with Zeke was appealing.

They were friends. Neither of them was looking for anything more.

"I'd like that."

Chapter 7

Daisy caught a reflection of herself in the mirrored door before stepping into the bowling alley. The combination of fitted dark-washed jeans and a burgundy polo shirt, paired with statement flats and jewelry, was the perfect outfit for the occasion. She straightened her blouse and walked inside.

Heavy thuds of bowling balls hitting the polished wooden lanes greeted her inside. Occasional bursts of cheers, laughter, and conversation created a fun and lively environment.

League and event posters lined the walls. Daisy paused to read the Sickle Cell Anemia poster. In addition to the admission price, 50-50 tickets were being sold as an extra stream of income toward the fundraiser. After making a mental note to purchase a few before leaving, she joined the eager customers waiting in line at the crowded customer service counter. A young African American woman wearing box braids assisted patrons with tickets, and a young red-haired Caucasian gentleman assisted others with shoe rentals.

Daisy hadn't been waiting long before she felt a gentle tap on the shoulder.

She turned to see Zeke looking like the cover feature of *People* magazine's sexiest man alive issue. She appreciated the outline of his toned shoulders peeking through his fitted white Polo shirt. His pair of starched and ironed jeans was evidence of the years he'd spent in the Marine Corps.

"Hi," said Zeke. "You look amazing."

"Thank you. You don't look too bad yourself."

"Thanks. I'm glad you made it. I've taken care of your charges. All you need to do is pick a pair of bowling shoes." He flashed her a happy smile.

"Thank you," she said, returning the gesture. "But this is a charity event. Aren't the entry fees part of the fundraiser?"

"Somehow, I knew that would be your response. Since you are here at my invitation, I took the liberty of purchasing your ticket. From what I understand, there'll be other opportunities to donate during the event." He placed the ticket in her hand and gestured toward the line for shoe rentals.

"Thank you. But next time it's on me."

"Fine with me as long as there'll be a next time."

Her heart skipped a beat. They were here to support an important cause. Nothing more and nothing less.

After changing her shoes, Daisy followed Zeke past rows of long polished lanes with gutters. Zeke stopped at lane twenty-seven. A charming couple snuggled up, leaning into each other as they shared quiet words and stolen glances.

"Hey, guys," said Zeke, interrupting their private moment. "I'd like you to meet my friend, Daisy."

The auburn-haired woman stood first. "Hi, Daisy. I'm Yolanda." She pointed to the tall, brown-eyed gentleman standing beside her. "This is my husband, Terry."

"Nice to meet you," said Terry, shaking Daisy's hand.

"Nice to meet both of you." She glanced from Terry to Yolanda.

Daisy looked at the large electronic player monitor displaying their names in vibrant graphics.

"Zeke told us you were coming, so we added your name to the roster. You guys are up first," said Yolanda, bouncing in her seat.

"Well, Daisy, it looks like we're teammates for the evening." Zeke smiled. "Do you bowl often?"

Daisy shook her head. "I used to but haven't in years. But I'm always up for a new adventure, especially when it's for a good cause."

"Don't worry. We'll be in this together. Besides, it's all about having fun, right?" He pointed to the ball rack. "Ladies first."

Daisy approached the rack. With careful consideration of the weight and size of the finger hole, she chose a comfortable ball. "Let's see if I remember how to do this," she said, playfully.

She stepped up to the lane, positioned herself, and with a deep breath, rolled the ball. It glided smoothly down the lane, knocking over six pins. Daisy turned back to Zeke with a satisfied smile.

"Not too shabby for a first try, huh?"

Zeke clapped his hands. "Well done! Now, let's do it again."

Daisy repositioned herself for the second turn. This time she knocked down the remaining pins.

"I can't believe it!" she said, throwing her head back in laughter.

"Great job, partner." Zeke's hand met Daisy's in a high five, but then he laced his fingers through hers, holding on longer than she anticipated.

"Now it's your turn." She smiled, releasing his hand.

Zeke aimed carefully for the center pin. It rolled straight down the lane, knocking over all ten pins. He turned to Daisy with a triumphant grin.

"Looks like we're off to a good start." He grazed her shoulder with his own.

The time flew by and after two exciting games, the score was tied. The lights of the bowling alley flickered as they prepared for a final frame of the tiebreaker. Cheers and laughter filled the air, but the atmosphere was tense with the score neck-and-neck. Daisy approached the lane, holding her breath as she released the ball. It slid smoothly, knocking over all ten pins.

"Eeeek!" She jumped and screamed with delight.

Zeke prepared for his final turn; Daisy sat nearby. He needed at least nine pins for them to win. Everyone fell quiet as he released the ball. It rolled straight for the pins, and with a resounding crash, hit nine.

Daisy jumped from her seat and sprinted toward Zeke. He spontaneously wrapped his arms around her waist. As if on cue, Daisy moved into his embrace. Slowly, she raised her eyes to his. A surge of unexpected emotions prompted her to retreat a step. Her heartbeat so fast she wondered if Zeke could hear its pounding.

"I apologize," he whispered. The soft words of regret contrasted the look of contentment in his eyes.

Daisy took another step backward and scanned the surroundings. Yolanda and Terry, deep in conversation, seemed oblivious to the emotional volcano that erupted moments prior. She took a deep breath. "No worries. We were caught up in the excitement of winning."

"I meant no offense," explained Zeke.

"None taken." Daisy glanced at her watch. "I should get going."

"Me, too."

They said goodbye to Terry and Yolanda, thanking them for a good time.

"How'd you find out about this charity event?" asked Daisy, as they changed shoes and gathered belongings.

"My business partner told me about it. I've always enjoyed giving back to the community. When I heard about this event, it seemed like the perfect opportunity. Plus, I like to keep busy. Keeps my mind occupied."

Zeke escorted her through rows of cars in the parking lot. Murmurs of conversations, punctuated by bursts of laughter filled the air as people walked to and from the bowling alley.

"I'm glad you came tonight. We should do this more often."

"I agree." Daisy covered her nose when the distinct odor of cigarette smoke wafted from a man walking past. "Did I mention that Liam was nominated for Entrepreneur of the Year?"

"No, you didn't. Congratulations to him and you."

"I had nothing to do with it." Daisy tilted her head slightly and smiled. "Liam's an astute businessman. He's more than doubled our customer base since taking the reins. He's increased revenue and reduced turnover. And I'm not saying this because I'm his mother. The records substantiate everything."

"I'm sure they do."

Daisy looked up to catch the emerging smile on Zeke's face. "The problem is, Liam doesn't believe he deserves the recognition."

"Has he seen the empirical data?"

"He has access to the same information I have. I'm pretty sure he's seen it."

"Maybe it would help if you showed it to him again."

"That's a great idea. I think I'll do that."

Since Harold's death, Daisy bore the weight of caring for her sons by herself. Of course, she brought their cares and concerns to God in prayer, and she planned to continue doing that. But it was nice to share her thoughts with Zeke.

Daisy tapped the car fob to unlock the door. Zeke quickly reached for and opened the door, waiting patiently while she adjusted herself behind the steering wheel.

Vroom! A powerful sound of a revving engine caught their attention as a motorcyclist raced past. Shortly thereafter, a high-pitched tire screech was followed by a heavy crash.

"Call 9-1-1," ordered Zeke. Then he closed the car door and ran toward the accident scene.

***

"9-1-1, what is your emergency?"

"There's been a motorcycle accident in front of Capitol Lanes Bowling Alley. Please send someone quickly."

After answering a few of the operator's questions, Daisy exited the Volvo and ran to join Zeke. A motorcycle lay on its side, visibly damaged with parts strewn across the pavement. The young motorist, still wearing a helmet, lay on the ground groaning in pain. The opened visor had been impaired. His ripped jeans exposed a significant, bleeding wound on his thigh. He groaned, and he was looking directly into Zeke's eyes as if pleading for assistance.

Zeke knelt beside the injured motorist checking for responsiveness and injuries. He nodded at her motion that indicated she'd called 9-1-1. She then stooped opposite Zeke, tenderly caressing the young man's arms.

"Can you tell me your name?" asked Zeke, in a calm and reserved voice.

"Leroy," the man whimpered.

"Hi, Leroy. My name is Zeke. Stay still, and try to remain calm. Help is on the way."

Leroy nodded. Confusion flashed across his face.

"Where does it hurt the most?" Zeke asked.

"My leg."

Zeke moved closer to the injury.

Daisy reached for Leroy's hand and offered a gentle squeeze. Peering into his anxious eyes, it was as if her sons were staring back at her. "Hi, I'm Daisy. I know you're in pain. We're here to help you." She offered a reassuring smile.

He locked eyes with her like he dared not blink. "Thank you."

"We need to elevate his leg." Zeke scanned the area looking for something useful.

"Try this." Daisy removed the strap with her free hand and gave him her purse.

"Uggh!" Leroy released Daisy's hand and groaned when Zeke lifted his leg and placed the purse underneath his thigh.

"You're doing great, Leroy," Daisy assured him. Take a slow deep breath for me."

She watched Zeke unbutton and remove his shirt, exposing his t-shirt. Then he pressed it down firmly on the wound with both hands.

"Are you coming from the bowling alley, Leroy?" asked Zeke.

"Yes, I work there." His words pronounced in jagged spurts. Each one ripped from his throat amid ragged breaths.

"Is there anyone we should call for you?" asked Zeke.

"My wife." Leroy's frown deepened.

Onlookers had gathered. Traffic slowed down in both directions.

"What's your wife's name?" asked Zeke.

"Tasha …" He started to speak, then paused, swallowed hard, and tried again. "Tasha. She's having our baby."

"That's wonderful. When is the baby due?" asked Daisy.

"Tonight!" Leroy's voice cracked. His eyes filled with concern. "I just got the call."

Leroy's declaration took Daisy by surprise. She squeezed his hand gently. She could only imagine the concern he felt for his wife and baby as he lay helpless.

Without hesitation, Zeke began to pray.

"Father, in the name of Jesus, we come to you on behalf of Leroy. You created him, and you know all about him. We ask that you heal his body from the crown of his head to the soles of his feet. Comfort him as the medical staff tends to his injuries. And,

Lord, please bless his wife, Tasha, and the baby that is on the way. We pray for a healthy delivery and that both mother and child will be fine. We pray that Leroy's injuries will not keep him from the birth of his child. And we ask these blessings in the name of Jesus. Amen."

"Amen," Daisy and Leroy responded in unison.

The faint sound of a siren rang in the distance.

"Do you hear that? Help is on the way," said Zeke, offering Leroy an assuring smile.

Leroy released a sigh of relief. "I'll give my wife a call when I get to the hospital. Thank you both for helping me."

When medical services arrived, Zeke provided them with all the relevant information about the accident. With Leroy safely in the care of the professionals, Zeke draped his arms across Daisy's shoulders, and they made a slow journey to the bowling alley parking lot. This time she was grateful for his calming touch.

"Are you okay?" he asked, as they neared her vehicle.

Unable to speak, she responded with a nod as tears sprang from her eyes. Her heart filled with emotion.

"Daisy?" His voice was charged with concern.

She paused, reflectively. "How'd you know what to do? Do you have medical training?"

"I received medical training in the Corps. The ability to perform emergency care was vital to our mission."

"What about you? Any training?"

"Not really. I learned CPR, but I cared for Leroy just as I would have cared for one of my sons."

"I believe it is a nurturing gift God gives to mothers."

As Zeke stood before her, his T-shirt streaked with blood, Daisy's heart stirred with a profound respect she hadn't felt before. He was brave, quick thinking, and remained calm under pressure. She hadn't felt such a connection with a man in a long time. Whatever it was, it was nice. And it was worth exploring.

Dusk settled over Tallahassee during Daisy's drive home. Light rays filtered through the trees as she drove into the entrance gate of Killearn Estates. An ambiance of peace descended over the subdivision while residents settled in for the night. She looked forward to unwinding after her adventurous evening.

Daisy spotted Donnie's car parked in the driveway.

Wonder why he didn't pull into the garage. Maybe he plans on going back out later. It's Friday night. Maybe he has a date.

Daisy lowered the driver's side visor. With one tap on the remote, the garage door sprang to life. The unfolding door panel revealed Liam's SUV resting inside. Both her sons were home. That's when she realized she hadn't checked her phone for messages. A barrage of questions was sure to ensue when she entered the house.

She grabbed her purse and exited the car. The door flew open before she took a step forward. A scowled-faced Liam appeared with one hand in each of his pant pockets.

"Mom, where have you been?" he asked, sounding like the father of a teenager arriving home after curfew.

She kissed his cheek and smiled. "I'm fine. You're home early. Didn't expect you until tomorrow."

He stepped aside so she could enter the house. Then he followed her into the kitchen. Donnie stood, leaning against the kitchen counter, wearing the same scowl as his brother.

"Plans changed. Lorraine and Dee have something to take care of for the engagement party, so we headed home early," said Liam. "What happened to you?"

"What do you mean? I went bowling; that's all." She looked down at her disheveled clothing. She could only imagine what her face and hair looked like. In all the excitement, she hadn't thought to check the mirror.

Donnie moved in closer. "You look like you went through a wind tunnel or something. What happened?"

Daisy placed her purse on the table and sat down. She relayed the moments leading up to and after the motorcycle accident, omitting details that included Zeke.

"That was nice of you to help, Mom. I'm sure it was unsettling," said Liam, taking a seat next to her. He gently touched her hand.

Donnie walked over to Daisy, leaned down, and kissed the top of her head. "Would you like a glass of water?"

"That would be nice. Thank you."

Donnie retrieved a glass from the kitchen cabinet and filled it with ice and water. Then he placed it on the table next to Daisy.

"Thanks," she said, taking a sip. "Sorry, guys. I was focused on the young man and didn't think to check my phone."

"I understand," said Liam. "But next time, please try to remember to call."

"Yes!" Donnie shook his head in agreement. "We had no idea what was going on."

"I promise to answer all your questions. But I'd really like to get some rest. I'll catch you up on everything tomorrow." Daisy stood, strapping her purse over her shoulder.

"Sure. We understand," said Liam.

After bidding them good night, Daisy made her way down the hall.

Talk about an emotionally packed evening. I hope the young man made it in time for the birth of his baby. And I pray that mother and child are fine. They'll have an interesting story to share with the child about the night of his birth.

Daisy entered her bedroom, removed her phone from her purse, and fell into the Queen Anne chair.

Three missed calls from her sons.

I know Liam and Donnie were worried when I didn't return their calls. The last thing I want to do is cause concern.

Her phone pinged and a text from Zeke appeared: **JUST CHECKING TO SEE IF YOU MADE IT HOME SAFELY.**

She replied: **MADE IT HOME SAFELY. LIAM'S BACK. HE AND DONNIE HAD QUESTIONS.**

She removed her shoes while waiting for his response. After a few seconds, he replied: **OF COURSE THEY DID. IF YOU WERE MY MOTHER, I'D HAVE QUESTIONS TOO. IT WAS AN EVENTFUL NIGHT, WASN'T IT? SWEET DREAMS. I'LL CALL YOU TOMORROW.**

The thought of chatting with Zeke again made her heart skip a beat. She couldn't deny the connection. He was easy to talk to. She was amazed at how effortlessly they got along. Being with him made her feel alive, but she needed to control her feelings.

Chapter 8

"This will get them out of bed."

The kitchen burst with familiar aromas of sizzling bacon, buttery pancakes and freshly brewed coffee drifted.

"They've never been able to resist a fresh home cooked meal." Daisy took a sip of coffee before placing a hand on one hip.

She woke early to prepare breakfast for her sons. They would be anxious to hear more about how she helped the motorcyclist the night before. She removed the last few pancakes from the griddle when Donnie entered the room. He paused momentarily, watching his mother work.

Daisy smiled.

He moved toward her. "Good morning," he said, kissing her cheek.

"Good morning. I knew the aroma of breakfast cooking would get you guys out of bed. I suspect your brother will soon emerge."

"You're probably right." He smiled, searching the cabinet for a coffee mug.

"I know my boys."

Within minutes, Liam appeared. "Good morning, everyone."

Daisy and Donnie exchanged glances and broke out in laughter.

"What's so funny?" asked Liam, kissing his mother on the cheek.

Donnie pressed the start button on the Keurig. "Mom said you'd be up soon."

"I couldn't help myself. Mom hasn't made breakfast in a while. I wasn't going to miss out on this."

Daisy's eyes sparkled as she listened to her sons. She enjoyed creating meals for them. Although, she didn't cook as often as she did when they were younger. It was a chore keeping a hungry husband and two growing boys fed. Their stomachs never seemed to fill. As soon as one meal was done, it was time to prepare the next one. But it was more than the body's satiation that kept her cooking. It was the appreciation and gratitude displayed for her time and effort. Liam and Donnie often made special requests for their favorite meals. And Harold bragged about her culinary skills to family and friends.

Daisy's phone pinged.

"You two go wash your hands. Breakfast is almost ready," she said.

Both men disappeared and Daisy glanced at the text from Zeke: **GOOD MORNING. I THOUGHT YOU'D LIKE AN UPDATE ON LEROY. HE'S THE PROUD FATHER OF AN EIGHT-POUND BABY BOY. MOTHER AND CHILD ARE FINE. LEROY ARRIVED IN TIME FOR THE DELIVERY.**

She replied: **THAT'S GREAT NEWS. PRAISE GOD!**

"Everything smells good," Donnie called out as he entered the room. "I can't wait to eat."

"Bet it never smells like this at your place," teased Liam.

"Maybe not," said Donnie giving Liam a side-eye. "But you can't take credit for the way it smells in this house."

Liam threw his hands up in agreement. Then he stepped closer to his mother and removed a serving tray from her hands. "Thanks for cooking. Donnie and I will do the dishes."

"We will?" asked Donnie.

Liam placed the dish on the table and nudged his brother on the shoulder. "Of course, we will."

Daisy's phone pinged again. She glanced at Zeke's message: **WOULD YOU LIKE TO JOIN ME IN A VISIT TO THE HOSPITAL LATER THIS AFTERNOON?**

The offer enticed her. She welcomed the opportunity to spend time with Zeke. He was extremely attractive, rather amusing, level-headed in a crisis, and wore a smile that was …

"Mom? Did you hear me?" asked Liam.

Daisy snapped back to reality and noticed both sons sitting down at the table ready to eat.

"I'm sorry. What did you say?"

Donnie looked at his mother with curiosity. "I said we'll take care of the dishes."

"That's great." Daisy tapped a quick response to Zeke letting him know she would love to join him.

She slid into a chair between her sons. Liam blessed the food and everyone dug in.

"Don't keep us waiting any longer," said Liam, cutting large chunks in his pancakes and dousing them with syrup. "Finish telling us about what happened last night."

Daisy recapped the story. Both men said how proud they were of their mother and both voiced their opinion about her stopping to help someone when she was alone at night.

Daisy took a sip of coffee and then turned to Liam, "How are things going with the workforce capacity issue?"

"I've been busy. It's hard to find time for future outcomes with looming deadlines and constant fires."

"Workforce is a valuable asset," added Donnie.

"Yes, it is. But it's employees like you who don't show up for work when they are scheduled to be there that make it difficult for all of us." Liam jutted his chin out, referring to an incident that occurred a week before.

"Are you going to bring that up again?" Donnie pointed his fork in Liam's direction. "I already apologized for calling in last week. I had rehearsal."

"I wish running a business were as simple as putting on a show," said Liam, his tone spiked with sarcasm.

"You don't know anything about what it takes to put on a show," Donnie said, irritation evident in his voice.

Daisy struggled to remain quiet. It was heartbreaking. She loved her sons so much. If things continued to escalate, breakfast would be ruined. "Perhaps, we can find a time that's best for all of us. I'll work on that when I get back to the office."

Liam looked in the distance and sighed, "I suppose that will work."

Neither son looked particularly pleased, but Daisy was happy. Crisis averted. She turned to Donnie, "Did Liam tell you he was nominated for Entrepreneur of the Year?"

"No, he didn't," Donnie said. He looked over at his brother. "That's great. Why so secretive?" He grabbed a crispy strip of bacon and crunched it.

"No secrets here. I haven't done enough to deserve the award, let alone the nomination." Liam's shoulders stiffened, and his face scowled. "So, I didn't bring it up. Dad built this business!"

"Isn't the award for this year?" asked Donnie.

"Yes, it is. I tried to tell your brother that." Daisy took a small bite of her pancake.

Liam puckered his brow. "It doesn't matter. Even if by some longshot, I received the award, I'd turn it down."

Daisy dropped her fork and placed her hands on her hips. "You will do no such thing. Your father would be disappointed to hear you were even considering turning it down."

"Set your ego aside, man. Think about it. This entire process is good for business," Donnie said sarcastically.

Liam's nostrils flared with annoyance. "What do you know about business? You spend your days pretending to be someone else while the rest of us handle the business."

Daisy wished she could send them to their rooms like when they were younger. She understood both of their perspectives. Maybe she could get them to understand each other's as well.

She raised one hand in the air. "That's enough. Stop it before you say or do something you'll regret," she said in an authoritative tone. "Liam, you're correct. Your father put everything he had into building this company for his family. He wanted us to reap the rewards of his labor. And he would be very proud of the work you've done since he died."

She turned to Donnie. "You're also correct. The nomination and the award would be great for Whittington Landscaping. It'd increase our credibility, enhance visibility, and it'd create a marketing boost."

Several expressions raced across her face. "Now let's finish eating. I've got places to go and people to see," she said, leaving no room for negotiation.

***

Later that evening, Daisy stepped into the Tallahassee Memorial Alexander D. Brickler, MD Women's Pavilion. The state-of-the-art medical facility was named in honor of a prominent African American obstetrician and gynecologist. In 1957, Dr. Brickler joined forces with his father-in-law to open Anderson-Brickler Midwifery and Obstetrical Services. He also worked at FAMU Hospital, the only place in Tallahassee where blacks could receive medical care in the Jim Crow South. A descendant of Harriet Tubman, Dr. Brickler, delivered over thirty thousand babies in his career.

She checked in at the security desk. Glancing around the spacious atrium, she spotted Zeke standing at the elevator.

"Zeke." His name fell from her lips with fondness.

He turned toward the sound of her voice. His eyes held hers with such affection that she couldn't look away.

"Hello, Daisy."

She watched his long strides quickly close the distance between them.

Their arms formed an uncomfortable embrace after moving awkwardly around each other. He patted her back clumsily, and she reacted with a mangled squeeze. When they finally pulled apart, she released a shy grin.

"You look amazing," he said, lightening the atmosphere.

"Thank you," she muttered. "You look nice, too."

"Are you ready to see Leroy and his family?"

"Yes. I'm excited for them. Do you think the gift shop is open? I'd like to purchase a few things before we head to the room."

"It's right around the corner. Let's check it out."

They followed the signs leading to the gift shop. Tall glass walls exposed various flowers and plants, balloons, and stuffed animals. When they entered, a soft sweet aroma of fresh flowers, an array of magazines, books, snacks, beverages, and sundry items filled the small but quaint space.

"Whoa!" said Zeke. "There's a lot of stuff in here."

"Not to worry. I came prepared." Daisy reached into her purse and pulled out her phone. "I have a list."

He chuckled. "I'm glad because I have no idea what to buy."

"Haven't you shopped for a mother and newborn before?"

"My wife was in charge of that. And then my daughter took over the responsibility."

Daisy liked the way they talked about their deceased spouses without feeling awkward.

Reaching for a hand-held shopping basket, Daisy prepared for a spree. As if on cue, Zeke grabbed one as well. He headed for the stuffed animals while Daisy browsed the books and magazine section. She picked one with an interesting cover.

"Hey Mrs. Whittington."

Daisy's eyes widened with recognition when she turned to see Gloria Jean standing a few inches away. She'd been so occupied with choosing a good book for Leroy's wife, she didn't notice anyone else.

"Hi Gloria. What are you doing here?" Daisy forced a smile and straightened the edges of the book in her hand that didn't need fixing.

"I work here, remember?"

Daisy glanced toward the door. "Oh, that's right. I forgot."

"Sometimes I like to browse the gift shop on my break. What about you? Is everybody alright?"

"Yes, I'm visiting friend. But thanks for asking." Clearing her throat, Daisy continued. "Listen, about the other day at the park…"

"That's none of my business." Gloria Jean held her hand up gently. "I'm not like some of the nosy sisters at the church. You do you. And Mrs. Whittington?"

"Yes?"

"It's good to see you smiling again." Gloria Jean offered a reassuring smile and placed the magazine back on the rack. Then walked out the shop.

Daisy exhaled deeply, anxiety evaporating from her shoulders. She continued shopping. Before long and Zeke had two bags full of gifts for Tasha, the new baby, and even a little something for Leroy.

"How did you find him?" she asked while they stood waiting for the elevator.

"Remember last night Liam told us which hospital his was in?"

"That's right."

They looked at each other for way too long and Daisy was relieved when the elevator arrived because she felt herself leaning toward him. The two stepped inside and the doors slid shut with a soft ding, closing off the outside world. The air grew thick with unstated tension.

Daisy's heart pounded in her chest. She stole a glance at Zeke while fiddling with her purse strap. His strong jawline and confident appearance sent a strange electric current through her body. What was that all about? Zeke turned as if to say something. Their eyes locked for an adrenaline-charged moment. When the doors finally opened, tension dissipated like air through a small hole in a deflating balloon.

Soothing shades of brown and cream covered the walls. Pink and blue balloons decorated the nurse's station. Walking side-by-side with Zeke, she scanned the art displays of various women and their health journeys. Busy hospital staff moved about the halls checking on the well-being of mothers and babies.

Blissful laughter poured from the slightly opened door at room 214. Zeke gave Daisy a quick smile before knocking.

"Come in," sang a joyful female voice.

Zeke held the door and waited for Daisy to enter, then he followed. Leroy sat in a wheelchair next to the bed where his wife lay with her head slightly elevated. On the other side of the bed, sat a clear hospital bassinet. The newborn rested, swaddled in a blanket.

"Leroy, hello. Do you remember us?" asked Zeke.

"How can I forget?" he said, struggling to stand.

"Please don't get up!" said Zeke, placing the bags on a nearby table and rushing to shake his hand. Daisy leaned in for a hug.

Leroy turned to his wife. "Honey, these are the people who came to my rescue last night. Meet my wife, Tasha."

"Nice to meet you, Tasha. I'm Zeke. Congratulations." He extended his hand for a shake. "And this is Daisy."

Daisy copied the gesture. "Glad to meet you, Tasha. How are you feeling?"

Tasha fiddled with her hair. "A little tired, but I'm fine. Thank you both for what you did for Leroy. I don't know what would have happened if you weren't there," her voice trembled, and she looked away.

Zeke placed his right hand over his heart. "I thank God for putting us in the right place at the right time."

"I agree," said Daisy. "Now tell us about your new addition."

A bright smile spread across Tasha's face. "He's eight pounds nine ounces of something special. He's sleeping now, but you can come around and take a closer look if you like."

"I thought you'd never ask." Daisy hurried to the bassinet like her feet were on fire. Zeke followed. Instinctively, he placed an arm around Daisy's shoulder as they observed the newborn.

After a few moments of utter adoration, Daisy turned to Tasha. "Aww. He's adorable."

"Yes, he is." Zeke gently caressed Daisy's shoulders and then led the way back to their spot at the foot of the bed.

"Thank you. We think he's the most beautiful baby ever!" Tasha smiled from ear to ear and then struggled to adjust her position in bed.

"What's his name?" asked Daisy.

With eyes filled with affection, Tasha turned to her husband. "Leroy Junior."

"But we'll call him LJ," said Leroy.

"Are you in pain?" asked Daisy, responding to the grimace when he shifted in the wheelchair.

"A little. My doctor said it was a soft tissue injury. But it's nothing compared to what Tasha went through," he said, glancing at his wife.

Tasha turned to Daisy. "How long have you two been married?"

Daisy dismissed the comment with a wave of her hand. "Oh …We're not … together … married." She looked to Zeke for assistance. He stood with a silly grin.

Tasha drew her brows together. "I'm sorry. I just assumed. You two seem so … together."

"No apology necessary," said Zeke, turning his attention to Daisy. "We're friends, but who knows what the future holds?"

"Honestly, Zeke!" Daisy gave an embarrassed grin.

A moment of awkward silence fell in the room.

"Please have a seat," said Tasha, quickly changing the subject.

Zeke held one of the vacant chairs for Daisy, and he sat in the other. They chatted about the events surrounding the birth and future plans. When Leroy Junior opened his eyes for a few moments before falling asleep again, they discussed who he resembled the most.

Then Daisy noticed Tasha struggling to keep her eyes open. "We should let you get some rest."

Zeke turned to Leroy. "Would you allow me to pray for your family before we take off?"

Leroy nodded in agreement. "Please do. And I appreciated your prayer last night. Thank God you both were there."

"God has perfect timing," said Daisy as they moved in closer to join hands.

Zeke prayed, "Heavenly Father, thank You for the miracle of little Leroy Junior. Be with Leroy and Tasha as they begin a new way of life. Guide them as they learn to care for little LJ.

Your perfect love demonstrates to us how to love our children. Teach them how to love like You.

Thank you for the privilege of parenthood and for being our perfect father.

And Lord, we pray for total healing and restoration for Tasha and Leroy. We ask You to bring relief from pain and restoration of health.

In Jesus' name, we pray. Amen."

Leroy nodded with appreciation, "Thank you, sir."

Tasha's mouth stretched into a full yawn. Daisy turned to Zeke, motioning in Tasha's direction.

"We should get going," she whispered.

"I'm so sorry. You guys don't have to leave," said Tasha.

"No need to apologize. You should try to rest when the baby's sleeping. But I'll leave my contact information so we can keep in touch." Daisy pulled a card and a pen from her purse. "I'll write my cell number on the back. Please call me if you need anything."

She placed the card on the table next to the gift bags.

Tasha released another yawn, before speaking. "Thank you both for the presents. I'm sure LJ will love them."

Zeke extended his hand in Leroy's direction. "It was our pleasure. Now you, take care of your family."

"Yes, sir. I will. You and your wife—friend have a free bowling night coming your way. Just ask for me at the front desk. I'll take care of it."

After saying their goodbyes, Zeke and Daisy walked out the door and down the hall.

"That was special," murmured Daisy.

"Yes, it was. I think we make a good team."

Soon, they entered the elevator, and Zeke pressed the button for the ground floor. Their eyes met.

The doors closed. Isolating them from the rest of the world.

Zeke continued, "It's hard to believe we only met a few weeks ago. I feel as if I've known you for longer."

"Strange. I feel the same way."

An unexpected bond had developed between them, and Daisy couldn't understand or explain it.

Zeke moved in closer as the elevator began its descent. He dropped his gaze to her lips. He leaned in, and she felt like she was hyperventilating. Thankfully, the elevator abruptly stopped.

The door opened, revealing a handful of people waiting to change places with them. Daisy wondered if the strangers could feel the passion in the air. It was a delightful mixture of excitement and nervousness. She stepped out of the elevator and wondered what would happen next after such an intimate moment that left her both giddy and hopeful.

Chapter 9

Two weeks later

The engagement party was in full blast when Daisy and Rosie stepped into the grand lobby with tall ceilings and large windows draped in elegant curtains. The aroma of fresh flower arrangements on sleek tables blended with the faint scent of polished wood. An assortment of perfumes and colognes lingered as guests walked past, their attire semi-formal, crisp, and immaculate.

The polished marble floor glimmered beneath the soft reflection of overhead chandeliers. Conversations hummed in the air along with glasses clinking and occasional bursts of laughter. A light jazz tune created a sophisticated ambiance.

Daisy, wearing a navy cocktail dress with tasteful lace details, led the way through the ballroom doors. Rosie, dressed in an elegant navy midi dress, followed close behind. A live jazz band stood on stage. A young saxophonist located front and center played solo. His cheeks puffed slightly as they blew into the mouthpiece. His fingers danced across the brass instrument, producing rich, sultry sounds.

Liam had reserved a spot for them at the front of the room. A pair of handsome young men ushered the ladies to their assigned seating past guests chatting, laughing, and mingling in small groups. Round tables with simple, elegant tablecloths scattered around a centered dance floor.

Rosie glanced toward the saxophonist. "He could give Kenny G a run for his money."

Daisy nodded. "Yes, he's really good."

"Donzel and I spent many nights making out in his old Chevy with Kenny G's soulful music bouncing from the speakers."

Daisy shook her head like she was trying to erase a visual of the couple in the backseat of a Chevy. "Seriously?"

"Of course, that was before either one of us gave our life to Christ. I'm glad Jesus didn't come back during my sinful days in college. I was that wretch they sing about in *Amazing Grace*."

Daisy's mouth hung slightly agape. Her eyes widened and her eyebrows shot up. "I get it. But did you have to say it like that? It doesn't work out like that for everybody. Some folks die in their sin."

"I know that, and I'm grateful. But I'm telling the truth. I was a handful, and you can see I'm still working on controlling the words that come out of my mouth."

Daisy attempted to change the subject. "Dee did a great job on the decorations. The room looks better than I expected."

"Hi, Mom." Liam beaming with joy, sauntered over. "I'm glad you're here. You look wonderful. Mrs. Rosie, thank you for coming. You look great, too."

Daisy smiled at him and Rosie nodded, telling him, "Thank you for inviting me."

"Of course. You're part of the family," said Liam.

Daisy took another quick glance around the room. "Honey, everything is beautiful."

He cocked an eyebrow. "Thanks. Would you like something to eat or drink?"

"We can take care of ourselves. You go find your fiancé and have a good time."

"Are you sure?" Liam asked, eyeing the floor.

Rosie waved in his direction. "You go on. I'll make sure your mother has a good time."

Liam looked grateful for Mrs. Rosie, which made Daisy happy. No doubt her son thought she would have otherwise been a lonely wallflower sitting alone all evening with little engagement with the crowd.

"Thanks. I think I saw her talking with one of my college frats. Can't let that conversation linger too long!" He grinned and scurried away.

"Look at that," Rosie pointed to the banner situated above the stage. "Liam and Lorraine: The perfect balance."

"What a clever message representing their journey together." Daisy hadn't known what to expect, but she was entertained by the fun-loving dancers who pirouetted around the floor. She looked forward to an amazing evening.

Rosie snapped her fingers to the beat of the music. "I didn't even know this place existed."

"From what I understand, it's changed owners several times over the last five years. The current owners did a complete overhaul. Lorraine fell in love with it, and I can see why." Daisy scanned the crowd. "This place is packed."

"Liam and Lorraine have a lot of people who love them."

Rosie's words put a smile on Daisy's face. "I pray they have a long and prosperous marriage. Oh, and lots of babies."

The band began playing, "How Sweet It Is." Couples all over the room made their way to the dance floor.

"That's my song," announced Rosie to everyone within earshot. Snapping her fingers to the rhythm of the beat, she rose and sashayed to the dance floor.

Daisy watched her lighthearted friend frolic with anyone and everyone in her path. That's when she noticed Donnie promenading in her direction.

"May I have this dance?" he beamed, extending a hand toward her.

Before she could refuse, he'd gently prodded her out of her seat.

Daisy flashed a forewarning smile, "Are you sure?"
"Of course."

"I don't think you're ready for this," she teased, hips shaking and hands flailing.

"Bring it on!" He beckoned as they made their way to the dance floor.

With confidence and grace, Daisy fluidly danced to the beat and energy of the music.

"That's my mama, y'all!" Donnie announced smiling.

Daisy couldn't believe her son put her on front street. She wanted to hide but the dancers started shouting and cheering, "Go, Mama! Go, Mama!"

Daisy pumped her hands in the air and beamed at the crowd.

Donnie's eyes filled with satisfaction and pride. He leaned toward his mother. "Okay, I see you. I didn't know you could dance like this."

"There are a lot of things you don't know about me."

"Let's keep it that way." He shook his head.

Soon Liam and Lorraine were on the floor dancing next to them. Both couples were swaying, cavorting, and laughing. When the song ended and the next one began, Liam exchanged places with his brother.

"My turn," he said. "And, Donnie, keep your hands to yourself."

"You can count on me, brother."

"I'm happy to see you having a good time," a smiling Liam told his mother.

"Are you surprised to discover I'm not an old maid?"

"Never thought you were an old maid. Just want to keep you under my watchful eye, that's all."

"There's one thing I need you to know."

"What's that?"

"I'm happy for you. Lorraine is a lovely woman, and she brings out the best in you. I only wish your father was here to share this moment."

"Me, too, Mom." He sighed. "Me, too."

They danced silently to the music until the song ended. By the time Liam led her back to her table, Daisy was breathless. She sat down next to Rosie.

"Would you ladies like something to drink now?" he asked.

Before they could answer, Donnie and Lorraine appeared with two glasses of ice water.

"We weren't sure what you preferred so we opted for water," said Lorraine. "We can bring something else if you like."

"This is perfect. Thank you," said Daisy, taking a sip. "Lorraine, this is my good friend, Rosie."

Lorraine nodded. "Nice to meet you."

"Thank you so much. Nice to meet you, too." Rosie took a sip. "Congratulations on your engagement."

A spontaneous grin stretched across Lorraine's face, and her eyes lit up. "Thank you."

Rosie paused between gulps. "I haven't danced like that in a long time. I'll be back out there as soon as I recover."

"Great. Save one for me," said Donnie, before heading back to the dance floor.

Daisy took another swallow before speaking, "Lorraine, are your parents here?"

"Yes, ma'am. They're around here somewhere." Lorraine's eyes swept the room. "I need to find them. When I do, I'll bring them over to say hello."

"Wonderful. It will be great to see them again."

"There they are," said Liam, pointing to a table near the front of the dance floor.

"We'll be right back." Lorraine laced her fingers into Liam's and pulled him away. The ladies watched the pair walk away. Lorraine waited patiently for her parents to finish a conversation with a young man. After a few moments, everyone including Liam and Lorraine burst into smiles and laughter. When they settled down, Lorraine said a few words to her mother, and the quartet made steps toward Daisy's table.

She stood as they neared. The women embraced one another.

"It's nice to see you. We must get together soon," said Helen.

"It's nice to see you too. How have you been?" said Lorraine's father. The six-foot-seven-inch podiatrist wore a salt-and-mostly pepper beard and a receding hairline.

"Doing well. Are you two enjoying the party?"

Helen shook her head. "Most definitely."

James grinned and shrugged his shoulders.

"Helen, James, this is my friend, Rosie."

Rosie nodded, "Pleasure meeting you."

After a brief discussion about the upcoming nuptials, James invited his wife to the dance floor. Liam encouraged his fiancé to do the same.

Although it was still early, Daisy felt exhausted and warm. To cool down, she suggested they make a trip to the ladies' room. The free-flowing air in the lobby was refreshing. Daisy swept her arm in a gentle arc. "I love the blue and gray colors in this motif."

Ignoring her words, Rosie pointed to the well-lit sign in the back of the lobby.

"The restrooms are around the corner," she said.

After taking care of their needs, the ladies washed their hands and freshened up.

"Am I going to have to ask, or are you going to give me an update?" asked Rosie.

"Update?" Daisy giggled. "What are you talking about?"

Rosie offered a probing glance, tilting her head, and raising her brows. "Your boyfriend, Ezekiel Daniel. You've been chatting with him on the phone for the last two weeks. You've gone bowling, and you saved a life. I feel like you're holding back."

"First of all, he's not my boyfriend." Daisy floundered through her purse, removed lipstick, and reapplied a coat. "And I'm not holding back? I'm holding it together. Let me see. He's a good listener, and he's very interesting."

"Yada, yada, yada. Has he invited you on a real date? What are you guys waiting on?"

"Yes, he asked me out to dinner several times. But I'm not ready for that. I like things just the way they are." She capped the lipstick and dropped it in the purse.

"And how long do you think he's going to be satisfied with being your little phone friend? You're two adults and allowed to go to dinner or a movie."

"I just don't want to start something I'm not willing to finish."

"What are you talking about? It's only dinner or a movie. He's not asking you to marry him."

"That's a good thing because I would definitely say no." Daisy leaned against the counter.

Rosie released a long sigh. "Evidently, you like something about him. You continue to chat with him on the phone." They walked out of the door. Daisy led the way back to the lobby.

"Okay. I like the feeling I have when I'm waiting for him to call. We have a lot in common and he makes me laugh. Above all, he loves the Lord."

Rosie paused, turning toward Daisy before entering the party. "You like him a lot, don't you?"

"Yes, but I also like my life as it is. I'm not ready to welcome anyone else into my circle. It's my safe place. It took me a long time to get here."

"Why are you telling me? You should be telling him."

"I don't plan on telling anyone. Some things you just must keep to yourself."

"You're going to have to do something. He's standing over there looking straight at you." Rosie pointed over Daisy's shoulder.

"What?" Daisy struggled to keep her expression neutral but was betrayed by the warmth creeping up her neck. Straightening her posture, she pasted on an air of indifference. She turned to see Zeke standing just inside the entrance of the building. He wore a pair of dark-washed jeans and a well-fitted white polo shirt. His dark eyes softened as they settled on her.

A glimmer of surprise filled his gaze, but it disappeared quickly, replaced by something warmer. Zeke slanted his head slightly as if trying to figure out what she was thinking. A slow smile tugged his lips.

"Don't freeze up now. Go talk to the man," said Rosie, turning to rejoin the party.

Daisy advanced toward Zeke.

"You look stunning." His hands clenched at his sides. His eyes held hers with fondness.

"Thank you. What are you doing here?"

The memory of the night in the elevator returned with potency.

"This is my building. My partner and I own it."

After her initial surprise, Daisy's face broke into a wide impressed smile. "I didn't know that. I'm here for my son's engagement party but I'd love a quick tour."

Fighting back a smile, he yielded. "Sure. This building has three ballrooms."

"Really? When I visited the building with my future daughter-in-law, we only looked at one ballroom. I guess she had made her decision by then."

"Come on. I'll show you."

In his element, Zeke deepened his voice, "The Elegant Event Center is both sophisticated and versatile. It features three exquisite ballrooms, each uniquely named and decorated to provide distinct atmospheres for different occasions. Two of them are currently occupied. This is the Crystal Ballroom," said Zeke, pointing to the room where Liam and Lorraine's party was still going strong. "We call it the crown jewel because of the chandeliers, elegant draperies, and mirrored panels."

"Very nice. Didn't you wonder if this was our party when you saw the name Whittington on your roster?"

"I didn't see the roster. My partner handles those things. Are you happy with the facilities? Is there anything you need?" He eyed her.

"No, everything is fantastic."

They strolled down the hall to a closed door labeled Opal Ballroom. The sound of Mariachi music oozed from inside.

He pointed. "This room features sleek, contemporary furnishings, and subtle lighting. Perhaps you can stop by sometime during the day when it isn't occupied so you can see inside." Evidently Zeke wanted to see her again.

She shrugged. "That would be nice."

Without objecting, she allowed him to loop her arm around his.

Zeke steered her down the hall to the last room. "This is the Radiance Ballroom. It features rich wood paneling, plush carpeting, and soft, ambient lighting. It includes a stage and advanced audiovisual equipment."

"I love the building décor," said Daisy. "Rosie and I were just discussing how beautiful the lobby and the ladies' room are."

Stuffing both hands in his pockets, Zeke crumpled his lips. "I can't take credit for any of that. We hired a professional to take care of everything. My office is around the corner if you'd like to see it."

Daisy nodded in agreement. Zeke led her around the bend.

"After you," he said, holding the door for her to precede him into his office.

Daisy studied the wall shrouded with a large encased American flag, a photo of a Marine Battalion, several citations, and various awards.

"Wow!"

"It's called a *Love Me Wall*. Every Marine has one in their office."

"Impressive."

"Thank you."

A framed photo displayed on the large oak desk in the center of the room caught her eye. She recognized Zeke in the picture.

"That's me with my daughter, son-in-law, and granddaughter."

"You have a lovely family."

"I think so," he said, eyes glistening with pride.

"I should get back to the party."

"You're probably right."

The two headed in the direction of the festivities.

"Do you check on all the events held in your buildings?"

"No, not at all. We have someone on duty. I left some paperwork in the office earlier, and that's why I'm here tonight. It was a pleasant surprise to run into you."

"I feel the same way."

He stopped, turned to her, and smiled tenderly. "I want to kiss you."

Her lips parted in consent.

His mouth settled over hers, sending her heart soaring. Zeke's hands traveled gingerly down her spine pausing at the curve of her back. He kissed her again softly at first, then deeply. After a few moments, he released her.

Daisy's heart raced; each beat echoed with exhilaration.

"Have dinner with me," he whispered in her ear.

"What?"

"Would you allow me to take you to dinner?"

Daisy recalled Rosie's warning. Zeke wasn't going to settle for being her phone friend. It was naive for her to expect him to do so. "You mean like a date? I'm not sure ..."

"Then a movie. We can drive there in separate cars. Anything to make you comfortable."

Clunk! Clunk!

Daisy jumped at the sound of footsteps in the distance. She glanced at her watch and realized she'd been gone for quite some time. Liam and Donnie probably put out an All-Points Bulletin on her and the search party was nearby.

"Let's talk later. I think we should get going."

"Of course. I apologize for keeping you away from the party for so long."

They rounded the corner to find Liam bounding toward them.

"Mom? Is everything all right here?" Liam's eyes darted from his mother to Zeke and back. His jaws clenched, and his muscles tightened.

"Of course. Liam, this is Zeke. Rosie and I met him at the Black Archives." Daisy attempted to calm her son with a tender smile.

Zeke extended his hand toward Liam. "Nice to meet you. I've heard a lot about you."

As if contemplating the gesture, Liam tensed his posture before shaking Zeke's hand. "I wish I could say the same about you. What are you doing in the back of this building with my mother."

"Mind your manners, Liam!"

"I understand your concern," Zeke said to Liam. "Daisy and I are friends."

"I ran into Zeke in the lobby," Daisy explained. "He told me he owned the property, and he was kind enough to give me a tour of the building. It's quite nice."

Liam said nothing.

"I hope you and your guest are having a pleasant evening," Zeke offered. "Please let me know if there's anything I can do to make it even better."

"We will." Liam wrapped his arm around his mother's shoulders. "Let's get back to the party."

Daisy searched Zeke's face for signs of disappointment or anger. She found none. "I apologize for the confusion. Thanks again for the tour. Duty calls. It was nice to see you again."

"No problem. It was nice to see you as well."

Liam scrunched his eyebrows and that infuriated Daisy, but she held on to her temper, knowing an argument would ruin the evening.

"Mom, you can't just wander off alone like that," said Liam, leading her back to the party.

"I didn't wander off. Rosie and I were in the ladies' room …"

"But Mrs. Rosie is sitting at the table now."

Frustration rose in Daisy's throat as she struggled to hide her anger. The last thing she wanted to do was create a scene.

"And now I'm going to join her," she said, leaving hastily.

Dropping into the seat next to Rosie, she muttered, "Liam has forgotten who the parent is in our relationship."

Rosie took a sip of water and shook her head. "He came looking for you earlier. I told him I'd seen you in the ladies' room, but I guess he thought you were taking too long, so he went to find you."

"He found me, alright. Does he think I'm a helpless old lady? If it weren't his engagement party, I would've told him a thing or two right then. He pulled me out of the lobby and sent me back in here like I was his child."

Rosie giggled. "Were you with Zeke?"

"Yes." Daisy's eyes drifted off into the distance.

"That explains his response. How did you expect him to react?"

Daisy rolled her eyes and huffed. "I didn't expect him to be rude. It was embarrassing."

"Here, I brought you some fancy cheese and crackers. Try one, it'll make you feel better." Rosie slid a small saucer over to her friend, but Daisy didn't seem to notice. Her lips parted with a gentle sigh. She stared in the distance as if caught in a fond memory.

Rosie leaned into the table, grabbed a cheese cube, and tossed it in her mouth. "Did something happen with Zeke that I need to know about?"

"Why do you ask?"

"Because you're gazing into the distance with a silly grin on your face. Now give up the goods. What happened?"

"Oh, it's nothing. Zeke told me he owned the building, and he gave me a tour. It's nice."

"You expect me to believe a tour of this building put that smile on your face?" asked Rosie, pointing to Daisy.

Daisy hadn't realized how much she missed having male companionship. It was a bit overwhelming, but she was happy to have shared such a moment with Zeke.

A childish grin swept across Rosie's face. "You're attracted to him, aren't you?"

"I think I am. But it's just a nice friendship, and I don't want to disrupt my entire life. What would that say about my love for Harold? What would Liam and Donnie think if I started seeing someone? Would they be angry? How do I know they wouldn't end up resenting me for trying to replace their father?"

"Girrrl, you have more worries than a hooker during a police raid," Rosie scoffed. "What if your boys are happy for you?"

Before Daisy could respond, Donnie appeared at the table. "Mrs. Rosie, you promised to save a dance for me. I'm here to collect."

What a relief. As much as she loved Rosie, Daisy needed to unpack her feelings. Something was happening between Zeke and her. It'd been years since she experienced anything like this. Did she even know how to date?

And what about Liam's reaction to Zeke? What was that all about? Obviously, he didn't approve of her standing alone in the hallway chatting with a man other than his father. Was his reaction an indication of things to come? What about Donnie? How would he respond? Unquestionably, she was a grown woman, free to see whomever she pleased. The three of them had struggled to find a new normal after Harold's death. Who was she to cause a setback?

Chapter 10

Two more weeks slipped by, packed with indecision, before Daisy finally agreed to see a movie with Zeke. Truth be told, she was more excited about spending time with him than she was about seeing the film. Deciding on an appropriate outfit was a feat. It took more time for her to select what to wear than to drive to the cinema. She went through several wardrobe changes before settling on a pair of jeans, a white t-shirt, and a red blazer.

One look at the crowded parking lot, and doubt wormed its way into her heart. What if someone recognized her? How would she respond? Had she made the right decision to meet him in such a public place?

Zeke stood near the entrance, waiting for her. He looked handsome in a pair of jeans and a beige polo shirt. Spotting her vehicle, he ambled over. She watched his purposeful stride, back erect, shoulders straight, and head high. Daisy checked her appearance in the rearview mirror. Touch-ups would have to wait, Zeke was by the car.

He extended his hand for support as she exited the vehicle.

"Hello." He locked eyes with her.

"Hello. How are you?"

"I'm great. Been looking forward to this all week."

Me too. Daisy fidgeted with her purse strap, then decided to play coy. "This movie is supposed to be pretty good."

"I've heard the same thing. But I was referring to spending time with you. I've been looking forward to our time together."

"Aww, you're sweet." She searched the area for familiar faces but found none.

They proceeded through the crowded parking lot past moviegoers walking to and from the theater. Zeke reached for her hand, but she pulled away slightly.

"You're still nervous about being seen in public, aren't you?"

"I feel a little exposed. People may not understand if they see us together. I don't like gossip." She advised with a frown.

"People are going to talk whether you are out with me or not. Would you feel better if we left?"

"No, I wouldn't. Please don't take offense. I'm new at this."

"None taken." He beamed triumphantly.

They stepped into the spacious lobby. The high ceilings and open layout made it easy to navigate. The American Bistro Kitchen and Bar sat to the left as they entered. Zeke hovered his phone over the digital kiosk to scan their tickets.

"Would you like food from the Bistro or would you prefer something from the concession stand?" asked Zeke.

"Concession, of course. What's a movie without popcorn?" asked Daisy, relaxing a bit.

"With lots of butter. Linda liked to add a few jalapenos to hers. I never understood the combination."

"Harold sprinkled the cheddar cheese topping on his."

They walked together to the concession stand. Daisy glanced around, checking again for familiar faces. Zeke offered a reassuring smile.

"Did you and your husband come to this theatre often?"

"No, we didn't," she said, fidgeting with her purse strap again. "Harold and I did a lot of bike riding, hiking, and other outdoor activities. I've only been here a couple of times with friends from church. This cinema is relatively new. If I remember correctly, it opened in 2018."

Daisy decided on a small popcorn and bottled water. Zeke opted for a large popcorn and a large Coca-Cola from the fountain. After getting their snacks, they headed to the theater. He walked beside her, making sure to stay close but not too close, respecting her space. When they found the seats, Daisy took a deep breath.

Reaching over, Zeke gently placed his hand on hers. "Are you okay?"

"I'm fine. Thank you."

Eventually, her stress diminished with the dimming lights.

What's wrong with me? It's just a movie. Besides, Zeke is kind and thoughtful. He's going out of his way to make sure I'm comfortable.

Soon both were focused on the screen. A growing bond developed between them, despite her underlying nerves. Throughout the movie, she occasionally glanced at Zeke, finding solace in his calm demeanor.

An hour and a half later, credits rolled.

"That was a great movie," he said, standing. "Would you like to grab a bite to eat?"

"Thank you for the invitation, but I should get home. Liam and Lorraine are cooking dinner at my house tonight. And thank you for making me feel at ease today. I appreciate it."

Zeke smiled. "We're going through this together."

Daisy took a deep breath. She guessed that Zeke Daniel had his heart set on spending time with her. The problem was she didn't know if she was ready.

Chapter 11

Sunday morning, Zeke woke with Daisy on his mind. Her big brown eyes aroused him. Those eyes and her compassion wouldn't leave him. Then there was the way her cheeks filled with joy when she smiled. He couldn't resist the urge to return the gesture.

But what he valued most was her unwavering faith in God. He reflected on a portion of Matthew 18 verse 19, "For where two or three are gathered together in my name, there am I in the midst of them." Together, they could accomplish great things for the Kingdom.

He left the bedroom and entered the kitchen to start a cup of coffee with the Keurig. While waiting, he grabbed the phone and dialed Esther's number.

"Hi, Dad."

"Hello, sweetheart. I thought I'd give you a call before I left for church. How are you guys?"

"We're great. You sound good. What's going on?"

"Not much. Reservations for the venue are steady. I'm not sure if it is because the word is getting around or if our promotions are working. Either way, we're constantly booked with parties and other events." Zeke placed the phone on the table, tapped the speaker button, then turned to the Keurig, the low hum filling the silence as he retrieved his coffee.

"That's great, Dad. It sounds like you're making things happen in Tallahassee. Have you met anyone special?"

"I'm glad you asked. I've found someone whose companionship I really enjoy. Her name is Daisy, and she's brought a lot of joy back into my life. It's still early, but I wanted you to know that she makes me happy."

"That's wonderful. Why didn't you just tell me instead of giving me a business briefing?"

Zeke chuckled. "I don't know." He hesitated. "I guess I didn't want to share too soon. I met her about two months ago. We talk on the phone mostly. We've gone to a couple of events together. We had our first real date last night."

A silent lull fell over the phone.

"You know I loved your mother. When she died, I thought life couldn't get any worse. And when things did get worse, I decided I'd never let myself fall in love again."

"Whoa, Dad, slow down," Esther exclaimed over the phone. "You've only had one date. Are you saying that you're in love with her?"

"No," chuckling, Zeke took a sip of coffee. "That's not what I'm saying, but I could see myself falling in love with her. I'm willing to take a risk and see where it takes us. Does that make sense?"

Softening her voice, Esther agreed. "Yes, it does. With everything that happened after Mom died, I swore I'd never marry."

"But you did and now I have a son-in-law and a granddaughter. Daisy and I are getting to know each other better. Maybe it will lead to something more. I'm not sure, but I'm willing to take the risk."

"I'm happy for you, Dad. What's that Scripture you like to quote? Romans 8:28, "And we know that all things work together for good to them that love God, to them who are the called according to His purpose.""

"Thank you for the reminder, sweetheart." He grinned broadly, rubbing the side of his head. "Daisy is widowed also. We have a lot in common, and I look forward to introducing her to you one day."

"Sooner than later," said Esther, concern in her voice. "I think it's time for me to visit Tallahassee."

"Let's make it happen."

After chatting for a few minutes, Zeke disconnected the call, realizing it was time to get dressed for church. It saddened his heart to know that Esther had once closed her heart to love. *Thank You, Lord, for delivering her from that fear.* He had been concerned about how she would react, especially considering the information that surfaced after the death of her mother. He'd had open and honest conversations with Esther about his desire for companionship. Now he experienced a sense of inner peace for himself and his daughter. He planned to move forward with his life and enjoy whatever God had in store for him.

***

Daisy opened her eyes before the alarm buzzed. She swung her feet over the side of the bed and into a pair of fuzzy slippers. There was only so much time she could spend staring at the ceiling thinking about Zeke. The senior choir was scheduled to sing, and members were instructed to arrive early. Sister Betty Thompson, choir director, and self-appointed church manager was sure to confront anyone who arrived late.

After her morning hygiene routine and personal devotion which included a prayer for Sister Thompson, Daisy basked in the warm morning glow from the sun shining through the kitchen blinds. Minutes later, she sat at the table enjoying a flavorful cup of coffee. Except for the soothing hum from the air conditioner, the room was quiet.

Through the years, she'd sat at that same table, discussing matters of the heart with one or both of her sons. Somehow, they felt most comfortable chatting with her about those things. Now she sat contemplating her heartfelt issues.

I never expected to feel this way again. Zeke is smart and funny, and he smells good. He's patient and understanding about my feelings. I can't stop thinking about him.

She took a small sip of coffee, relishing images of their date playing in her mind.

"Good morning. You're up early."

Liam's greeting brought her musing to an abrupt halt.

"Good morning," she said, lowering her cup to the table. "I couldn't sleep, so I got up."

"Everything okay?"

"Yes. Have you and Lorraine decided on a date yet?"

"We've narrowed it down to winter of next year. A few months after Donnie graduates." Liam moved around the kitchen, making a cup of coffee.

Daisy wanted him to share more information. But instead, he stared into the Keurig like it held the answer to some kind of mystery.

"Is everything okay?" she asked.

"Sure, why?"

"Because you look like something's on your mind. Did you and Lorraine have a spat?"

Liam slid into the seat beside her. "No. It's just the opposite. We're fine."

"Then what's on your mind? Spit it out!" Daisy assumed it was about the extra time she'd been spending away from home. It was clear both sons were concerned about her whereabouts.

Liam lowered his eyes, then nodded. "Lorraine and I are looking at houses. We'd like a place of our own."

The announcement came as no surprise. Ironically, she looked forward to having the house to herself. How nice it would be to come and go without having to explain. She loved her son dearly, but Liam behaved like a helicopter parent.

"That's understandable," she said. "A wife should have a place of her own."

"I'm not abandoning you. We'll move somewhere nearby. And after his graduation, Donnie can move in here."

Daisy gasped. Had Liam lost his mind?

"What? Have you talked to him about this?"

"Not yet. But I'm sure he'll agree it's the best thing for you."

Daisy shot him a sideways glance. "Liam Whittington, you're not in control of everyone's life! Your brother is going to graduate and probably move to a place with opportunities for people in theatre. If that place happens to be Tallahassee, then great. But even then, he has no obligation to move in here. Where he chooses to reside is his decision. He has the right to pursue his dreams."

Liam released a distinct grunt. "I'm glad he's so passionate about the theatre; hopefully, it pays off someday."

"Where is this snide remark coming from? In the past, you were always supportive of your brother and his dreams for the future."

"I think it's time for Donnie to grow up." Liam's nostrils flared.

"I'm not having this conversation with you. And you will not guilt him into staying in Tallahassee or into moving in here with me. I'm not helpless. I have plenty of life left in me. Now if you will excuse me, I'm going to get dressed for church."

Daisy snatched her cup from the table and trudged out of the kitchen. Liam and Donnie got along with each other for the most part. Even as children, they didn't argue and fight often. And when they did, the argument never lasted more than a few hours. Harold had been determined that neither would go to bed angry at the other, demanding they talk it out until a meeting of the minds was formed. Some nights took longer than others.

Daisy set her cup down and prayed for her sons. Then she searched her closet for a dress for church. She couldn't believe Liam's audacity. But she was happy that he and Lorraine were moving forward with their house-hunting plans. Her emotions had been all over the place the last couple of days.
***

Betty Thompson stood front and center, facing the choir as she directed them to stand. Rising in unison, all three sections waited for the signal to begin. For the next few minutes, she joyously led the twenty-member choir in a beautiful rendition of Maurette Brown Clark's "Just Want to Praise You." Then suddenly, Sister Thompson raised her eyebrows and pursed her lips. Someone was off-key. Rosie nudged Daisy, who was standing next to her in the soprano section. Daisy refused to look at her friend. Making eye contact would only lead to an attempt to stifle a laugh.

Sister Thompson stepped closer to the sopranos and furrowed her brow in search of the culprit. Her eyes connected with Gloria Jean, standing on the other side of Daisy. The director motioned upward, asking Gloria Jean to go higher. When that didn't work, Betty subtly placed her finger on her lips, asking Gloria Jean not to sing.

Daisy felt another nudge from Rosie. This time, it nearly knocked her off her feet. A small chuckle escaped before she could smother it. Sister Thompson flashed a serious side-eye, prompting Daisy to regain her composure. Minutes later, the song ended, and the choir was seated.

Daisy caught a glimpse of Rosie's eyes sparkling with amusement and the corners of her mouth twitching. Rosie buried her head in her hand, shoulders shaking slightly.

Daisy scanned the congregation. Several others were giggling as well.

"I'm glad Sister Thompson asked Gloria Jean to stop singing," whispered Rosie, when she pulled herself together.

"Shh! This is not the time or the place." Daisy refused to be distracted. She came to church to hear from God, and that was what she planned to do.

Chapter 12

Two weeks later

"Which one?" Zeke looked into the camera of his MacBook.

"Black or blue suit?"

"Relax, Dad," said Esther. "I think the black suit and tie make you look like you're getting ready to serve communion. Why not wear a nice dress shirt and slacks?"

"Maybe you're right. This is overkill." Zeke eased into the corner armchair and repositioned the MacBook on the wooden side table. It was where he spent late nights in quiet reflection. He eyed the understated bedroom that he'd placed little effort into decorating.

"I'm glad to hear you've found someone you like. From what you've shared with me about Daisy, she seems to be a nice lady."

"I think so."

"Don't forget to call me when you get home. I want to hear all about it."

"Isn't that ironic? When you were a teenager, I was the one asking about your dates."

"True, but I thought you just didn't want me to have fun. Now I know you only wanted to keep me safe."

"That's right."

"I'm going to tell you like you told me way back then. Have fun but don't compromise who you are just to make someone else happy. God has a plan for your life."

"Thanks for the reminder, kiddo. I should get going. I'll call you later."

Zeke decided it was best to relax and have fun as Esther suggested. Even so, his stomach began rumbling like a property in the middle of renovation. Even when he arrived at Georgio's Fine

Food and Spirits, his stomach was in turmoil. He remembered how Daisy turned down his invitation to dinner several times before she finally accepted. Would she show up tonight or would she call at the last minute with an excuse? His pulse raced in anticipation of seeing her again.

Zeke beamed when Daisy appeared. His eyes trailed from the top of her salt and pepper tresses to the elegant form-fitting dress, down to her shapely calves. *Breathtaking.* He rose to meet her and directed her to their table. After pulling out her chair, Zeke returned to his seat.

"You look amazing," he said, gazing with appreciation.

"You look pretty good yourself."

A young blonde woman, holding two menus appeared, her singsong greeting sounded rehearsed. "Good evening, I'm Molly. I'll be your server. What can I bring you to drink?"

Daisy ordered water with lemon. Molly's request faded to the background as Zeke studied Daisy's lips. How could they be so perfectly shaped?

Daisy caught him staring when he failed to place his drink order.

"Zeke, she's asking for your selection?"

"Of course." Turning his attention to Molly, Zeke requested a tall glass of sweet tea."

"Mr. Daniel, were you staring at me?" Daisy asked as soon as the server left.

"I wasn't the only one. Practically every man in the restaurant had his eyes on you."

"You're exaggerating."

The server returned, placing the drinks before them. Zeke thanked her and then took a sip of tea before speaking. "You seem to grow more beautiful each time we meet."

"That would only be a total of four times."

"I'd like to change that," he gave her a mischievous smile. "Don't get me wrong, I enjoy chatting with you on the phone and texting you throughout the day, but it's nice to sit across from you at a dining table."

Daisy smiled. "Likewise."

"You surprised me when you accepted my invitation. I don't know which one was more difficult to do, getting you to say yes or knowing when to bid on a property."

Daisy giggled.

"How was your transition from military to civilian life? Were there many adjustments?" she asked.

"Let me count the ways," he smiled gently. Zeke leaned back in his chair with a distant gaze. "In the Corps, we worked on a rigid schedule. Some mornings, we were up before dawn, or 0'dark-thirty as we like to call it, for training. Then there was the dress code. Always in uniform and always inspection ready. And, of course, there was the comradery. Marines have a shared identity. We're brothers and sisters with one purpose."

"If things were so great in the military, why did you decide to retire?"

"Good question. It was beginning to put a strain on my marriage. Honestly, things were headed downhill before I considered retirement. Linda had been unhappy for a long time. I chose not to see it."

Daisy nodded but didn't respond.

"I think I mentioned we bought a home in Jacksonville. I hoped leaving the military, purchasing a home, and settling down would save the marriage, but it didn't. Things grew worse, and then the accident occurred."

"I'm sorry to hear that. You don't have to share if you don't want to. I understand it must have been difficult for both of you."

Her fingers slipped over his, deliberate yet hesitant, before settling in a soft squeeze. The sensation rushed through him, intense and sweet, a connection that was both a promise and a question. Then she let go. The loss left his skin cold, longing for her warmth. Zeke's gaze lingered on her hand—petite, steady, and yet trembling faintly as if it had betrayed her. When their eyes finally met, the gravity of what had passed between them hung thick in the air.

"I don't usually talk about it, but this feels good. I don't want to put a damper on the evening.

Molly reappeared and took their orders and the menus.

"I have a question for you," he said. "What took you so long to accept my invitation? I know I'm not the best-looking man in the room, but I can hold my own," he teased, and they both laughed.

"Well, I haven't seen every man in the restaurant, but I'd give you a ten." She giggled. "Besides, my hesitation had nothing to do with you and everything to do with me. I haven't felt comfortable enough to have dinner with any man other than my sons since Harold died."

"I get that. I'm glad you're comfortable with me." He took a sip of tea. "Liam seems to be protective of you or, at least, that's what I suspect."

"Yes, they both are."

Zeke detected a suggestive warning in her voice. He recognized it since he felt the same about his mother when she was living.

"How do you like working with your children?"

"I love it. I only work a few hours each day." Daisy took a sip of water and swallowed. "What do you like most about the real estate business?"

"It's different from anything I've ever done. I like having control of my time. I enjoy the process of finding properties and negotiating deals."

"Tell me about your relationship with God," requested Daisy.

"I owe Him everything. I don't know how I would have survived the things I've been through without Him. What about you?"

"I believe in God. I do my best to live a life that pleases Him."

Whew! Zeke was glad to hear that.

During the meal, he and Daisy talked about life goals and interests, retirement plans, family, and cultural interests. Time moved faster than either of them wanted or expected. After paying the tab, Zeke escorted Daisy to her car.

"Did you enjoy dinner?" he asked.

She nodded. "Yes, everything was delicious."

"Everything?" His eyes held hers with tenderness and reached for her hands. Just as he leaned in for a kiss, the sound of an approaching car shattered the moment. Daisy dropped his hand and took one step back.

Zeke's heart constricted from seeing her reaction. Not only because he wanted to kiss her, but he realized she may not be ready to move forward. They stood silent for a moment. The only sounds heard were the soft hum of engines and the faint footsteps crossing the parking lot.

Daisy unlocked her car door and edged into the driver's seat. He waited until she fastened the seatbelt to speak.

"You haven't told your sons, have you?"

"No, I haven't. Maybe we shouldn't tell anyone … yet."

For a fleeting moment, Zeke thought about Linda and the way their marriage had been a dirty little secret she kept from her boyfriend.

"I know we're still figuring things out, but if you're not prepared to be candid with your sons, are you ready to be with me? I told you I'd be patient, and I meant it, but that doesn't mean pretending we don't exist. If this is going to work, we need to be honest—not just with each other, but with the people in our lives."

Daisy stared off into space, her forehead wrinkled and she twisted a small piece of hair at the nape of her neck. "I'm not sure how my sons will react. They might not understand."

Is she ashamed of me, or is she still holding on to her past? Either way, I can't ignore the possibility that this is more than just hesitation—it's a wall she's not ready to tear down.

"Do you plan on telling them at all?"

"I'll give it a shot tomorrow. My sons were close to their father."

"And my daughter was close to her mother."

Zeke paused for her reply, but his thoughts kept coming. Was she truly concerned about her sons' reaction? Or was she using them as an excuse not to move forward?

"Like I said, I'll give it a shot."

Zeke nodded and closed the car door. Then he watched her drive away. The familiar feeling of rejection ripped through his core. He swore he'd never visit that place ever again. The last time he allowed himself to wallow in feelings of inadequacy, he'd nearly lost his mind. Was this the time to pump the breaks, make a one-eighty, and head in the opposite direction. Sure, it would be painful, but better now than later.

Zeke stood still long after Daisy's taillights disappeared, his hands dormant in his pockets, the taste of unfinished conversation lingered like footprints in the sand. There were things she wasn't ready to say, and maybe he wasn't ready to hear. Something changed and he wasn't sure if it was the beginning of something genuine or the start of a subtle withdrawel.

Monday morning began with small, unpredictable cloudbursts. At first, rain sprinkled like popcorn in the microwave–slow at first, then a few isolated showers. Then, suddenly, a downpour. Daisy stared blindly out her office window, thinking of Zeke. Like the popcorn showers, her emotions were sporadic—one moment euphoric and the next uncertain.

Zeke was adamant about not hiding their relationship. She wondered why his feelings had changed. In the beginning, he seemed to understand her reluctance about being seen together. Whatever his reasons, she agreed it was time to tell her sons she was seeing someone. That's why she'd told Liam and Donnie she wanted to talk to them about something over dinner. They agreed and Daisy had been in prayer ever since.

The morning moved quickly. She reviewed and confirmed the week's schedule for landscaping crews. Daisy made sure all jobs were assigned and changes communicated. Afterward, she met with Sophia to discuss the week's priorities, upcoming projects, and issues from the prior week.

After the meeting, Daisy checked the email on the company's shared drive. She clicked on the message from the Entrepreneur of the Year committee.

Subject: Congratulations on Your Nomination for Entrepreneur of the Year!

Dear Mr. Whittington,

> *We are thrilled to inform you that your nomination for the Entrepreneur of the Year Award has been officially approved and submitted for voting by the members of our business community.*

Warm regards,

Unable to conceal her delight, Daisy pushed back from her desk and skipped to Liam's office. It's a good thing his door was opened; otherwise, she may have broken it down.

"When's the last time you checked your email?" she asked, racing into his office with the printed acknowledgment. She sped around his desk and landed behind the chair where he sat. Daisy eyed the landscape design software on his computer screen.

He sighed.

"I take it you saw the email."

Liam continued to study the 3D rendering on his computer.

"Your nomination for Entrepreneur of the Year was approved, and now it's up to the locals to vote for you. I'm proud of you, son!"

"You know how I feel," Liam said, frowning.

Daisy had presumed Liam would change his mind about the situation. "We talked about this already," she said, walking around and standing in front of his desk.

His scowl deepened. "No, we didn't. You and Donnie talked. I'm not interested."

"Well, excuse us for thinking you deserve to be recognized. You've done a lot for the business and the community."

"Of course, you think I deserve it, you're my mother. And what does Donnie know about business. He's too busy perfecting his stage presence."

"I don't know what's really bothering you, but I can't talk to you right now."

"Nothing's wrong with me. Would you just leave things alone, Mom?"

Daisy opened her mouth. She wanted to say something but decided against it. She didn't understand her son's attitude. He obviously had a lot on his mind, and it was causing him to lash out. She'd keep quiet for now.

Besides, he was going to be Lorraine's husband soon. Marriage would be an adjustment. No need to add extra baggage. Later, she would take it to the Lord in prayer.

Daisy shrugged, attempting to de-escalate the situation. "Okay, then. I'll get back to work."

Daisy felt as though she was walking around in a fog for the rest of the day. She scheduled routine maintenance for a few of the company vehicles, contacted suppliers and vendors to confirm delivery times, and placed new orders. A few hours later, she headed out.

***

That evening, after sipping sweet tea on the sofa in the living room, Daisy decided it was time to treat her sons to a meal again. With an apron tied around her waist, she pulled the large pan from the oven. Hot and filled with savory spices, the lasagna was the same recipe her mother had used through the years.

Grateful their differences hadn't stopped the pair from working out together, she waited for Liam and Donnie to return from the gym. Daisy remembered how Harold would join the boys for their workout. She would have a hearty dinner prepared when they returned. Lasagna was Harold's favorite. Daisy didn't prepare it as often as she did when he was alive; but tonight, she planned to surprise the boys with their father's favorite meal complete with oven-roasted asparagus and freshly baked garlic bread. She had stopped by TC Bakery for a delicious red velvet cake for dessert.

It was those memories that kept the family together. It was also the reason Daisy was concerned about how her sons would react when she told them about Zeke. Tonight's confession was sure to change everything.

"Hey, Mom," said Donnie, entering the kitchen from the garage followed by his brother. "Do I smell lasagna?"

"Yes, you do. But it's competing with both of your armpits." She pinched her nose. "You guys must have had a good workout."

"Yes, we did! And we're looking forward to eating dinner," Donnie said, eyes wide and fixed on the pan of lasagna. His mouth flew open, and she thought his tongue would fall out. The only thing missing was his wagging tail.

"Thank God, we have more than one shower and plenty of soap," Daisy teased. "Everything's ready. We can eat as soon as you two get cleaned up."

Soon everyone was seated around the dinner table. Liam blessed the food. Donnie grabbed a fork and dug into the cheesy layers of meat and pasta. Liam stared at his plate, playing with a portion of his lasagna.

"Earth to Liam. Are you there?" she asked.

"Sorry." Liam squirmed in his seat. "Miss Anderson from Anderson Consulting stopped by the office this afternoon."

"Trouble at the office." Donnie smirked, then rolled his eyes. "That explains the way you played basketball today. I think you set a record for most airballs in a single game." Donnie blustered, like he'd won the fight. His smirk which irritated Liam, never left his face.

"I guess I'd have better shots if all I had to do was memorize lines all day," snapped Liam.

"My chosen profession has nothing to do with my ability to get the ball in the basket. You spent more time 'chasing' the ball than playing the game." He did air quotes around chasing, determined to aggravate his brother.

"What did Miss Anderson have to say?" asked Daisy, purposely changing the subject.

"She stated that the landscaping work at two of her locations was sloppy. She threatened to take her business elsewhere."

"We can't let that happen," said Daisy. Lifting her glass, she sipped some tea.

"I had Sophia schedule a meeting for us to meet with Miss Anderson in our office tomorrow morning at ten. After that, I'll meet with Grady and his field team. They're assigned to her properties." Liam placed a forkful of lasagna in his mouth.

"Great idea." Daisy smiled reassuringly. "Anderson Consulting has several offices in Tallahassee, and they are one of our key clients. I'm sure we'll get to the bottom of this and provide the service she's come to love and expect."

Donnie shook his head. "I have a research and script analysis in the morning." He shoved more lasagna in his mouth and swallowed.

"I assumed you wouldn't be available. I'm sure your acting skills will come in handy the next time we need to negotiate a contract," Liam spat out with annoyance.

Donnie turned to his brother. "Maybe you should have checked with us before you arranged the meeting."

"Do you think we should reschedule?" asked Daisy, studying Donnie's troubled face. "I'm willing to stay later if she can meet in the afternoon."

"That's probably not a good idea. She's already irritated with us. You and I can handle the meeting."

"Fine with me." Donnie shrugged his shoulders.

Daisy mustered a faint smile. "That's enough about business. Let's enjoy dinner."

"What did you want to talk to us about," asked Donnie, devouring a section of garlic bread.

That was her cue. It was now or never. Daisy contemplated all day about the best way to tell them about Zeke. Now she second-guessed her timing. Liam and Donnie were quarreling again. Perhaps she should wait until they both were in a better mood.

"I hope it's not about the nomination." Air filled Liam's chest as he waited for his mother to respond.

"Since you brought it up," Daisy said in a stern voice. "You can't just withdraw your name. It's the opportunity of a lifetime. Do you know how proud your father would be?"

Liam shook his head in opposition, irritated with his mother's words. "Like I said before, Dad is the one who built everything from the ground up. I'm standing on his shoulders. This nomination belongs to him."

Donnie stared at his brother in disbelief. "Dad was a great man, but he's gone. This is your moment, Liam. He would've wanted you to be recognized for your hard work and dedication. He knew you would do well. That's the reason he left you in charge."

"What hard work? What dedication? I'm following his blueprint. I've done nothing out of the ordinary." Liam pointed to his chest. "I was the one who hired the man that almost sent us into bankruptcy."

Daisy swallowed her fury. "And you were the one who saved the company by hiring an auditor. That was brilliant. I can't tell you the number of times your father and I made business decisions we later regretted, but he never gave up. Not even when *I* wanted to. Harold laid the foundation, but you've kept it standing and expanded it."

"That's no small accomplishment. The community sees something in you that's worthy of recognition," added Donnie.

Liam paused before speaking. "Don't you see? Every decision I make is about what he would have done. I feel like a phony being acclaimed for his work."

Daisy softened her tone. "It's not just his work anymore, dear. It's yours. You've put your mark on the business and brought in new ideas, and new energy. You've earned this."

"I don't want to betray his memory by accepting an award that should have been his."

"The way I see it, you aren't betraying his memory. You're acknowledging everything he taught you," said Donnie.

Liam took a swallow of tea before speaking. "I don't want people to forget what he did or who he was."

Daisy's heart plummeted. Her resolve to convince Liam he deserved the nomination battled with the admiration Liam felt for his father. "No one will ever forget your father. You have his strength and his vision, but you are your own person. This nomination is about that."

Liam wore a blank expression. Daisy couldn't tell if she had gotten through his stubborn blindness.

"Accepting this nomination," she continued, "wouldn't just be for you; it would be for both of you. It's a testament to everything you've both accomplished."

Liam locked eyes with his mother for a moment. "Okay, I won't withdraw my name."

Daisy's eyes smiled. "That makes me very happy."

"Me, too, bro," said Donnie, stuffing his mouth with a huge bite of garlic bread.

The remainder of dinner was lively, and conversation flowed easily around the table. Daisy enjoyed watching her boys enjoy their meal, laughing and chatting about old times. Bringing up Zeke now would change the mood of the room. Just the thought filled the pit of her stomach with nerves. What was she supposed to do? Why was she so anxious? A part of her wanted to announce to the world that she had found someone intriguing who reciprocated her interest. Part of her wanted to enjoy the time watching her boys, talking with each other like they did when they were younger.

Daisy decided to enjoy their time together. The sound of Liam and Donnie laughing made her heart sing. She took it all in. And now, she was going to relish this time with her sons without disturbing their peace. She would have that conversation with them tomorrow.

***

Too restless to watch TV, Daisy sat in her bedroom reading after dinner. She hadn't heard from Zeke since earlier that morning when she told him about her dinner plans. Perhaps he was waiting to hear from her. Mindlessly flipping the pages of the latest issue of Ebony magazine, she second-guessed her decision to delay telling her sons about Zeke. If only they weren't arguing so much lately, she wouldn't worry about adding to their stress. What was their underlying issue?

She recalled a time when they were younger. The boys were sitting in the living room watching TV. On her way to the kitchen for a glass of water, Daisy noticed the empty trash can without a trash bag inside. She'd been on the boys about completing their chores. So, she headed to the living room, grabbed the controls, and muted the TV.

It didn't take long for her to gain their full attention. "Who took out the trash today?"

"I did. Again!" Liam contorted his face.

Donnie threw up a hand. "It was my turn. I was supposed to do it, but Liam did it before I had a chance."

Liam cocked his head. "Yeah, but you were too slow. I didn't want you to get in trouble, so I did it."

Donnie frowned and rolled his eyes. "I was gonna do it. You always think you're better than me!"

Daisy moved to the couch and sat. Then she called the boys over. They stood in front of her. Sitting at eye level, she glanced from Liam to Donnie and back.

"Liam, it's important to let your brother take responsibility for his chores."

He nodded, slightly. "Yes, ma'am. But I didn't want him to get in trouble."

She turned to Donnie. "You need to be quicker next time. Now go put a trash bag in the trash can."

Imitating his older brother, Donnie nodded before responding. "Yes, ma'am."

She knew the spat had nothing to do with the chore and more to do with Liam feeling the burden of responsibility for Donnie. After a small chat with Harold, they addressed the real issue, and all was well between the boys. Harold made sure they talked it out until it was settled.

That was then. What was their current issue? And how could she help them come to a resolution?

Pulling her thoughts to the present, Daisy tossed her shoes in the closet. Next, she stripped off her clothes and slipped into a pair of silk pajamas. Just then, her cell phone rang and Zeke's name appeared on the screen. "Hello?"

"Hi, there. How are you?"

"Doing well." Daisy flopped onto the corner of the bed. "It's good to hear your voice."

He paused for a long moment. "I would've called earlier, but I had a late meeting with Arthur. It looks like we're going to close on the Bannerman property within the next week or so. How are you?"

"I'm fine. That's great news! Happy for the both of you."

"Thanks."

"I also have good news to share." She walked over to look out the bedroom window. Opening the blinds, she peered into the darkness. "Liam agreed not to drop out of the running for Entrepreneur of The Year. He doesn't know it, but I plan to start campaigning for him tomorrow."

"Good." Zeke's response was curt and detached.

Daisy hesitated. She could tell something was wrong. He probably wondered about the discussion she was supposed to have with Liam and Donnie. After an awkward moment, she attempted to chat once more. "I'm going to have flyers printed. Then I'll take them around to some of the small businesses in town. I thought maybe you'd like to join me," she said, attempting to bring him into the conversation.

"Sure. I'll help." She expected him to be more enthusiastic, but he wasn't. Something in his voice troubled her. She couldn't ignore it any longer.

"Zeke, what's wrong?" Daisy braced herself for the answer.

"What makes you think something's wrong?"

"I can hear it in your voice."

Zeke cleared his throat before speaking. "Okay. I hoped you would tell me before I had to ask. Did you talk with your sons about us?"

Dread struck her stomach. "Not tonight. There's this palpable tension between them. I don't want to create additional pressure for them. I'll tell them, but not now." She tried to sound optimistic.

"Daisy, I enjoy spending time with you. I haven't felt this way about anyone in a long time."

"Yes, and I feel the same way. I didn't think I would ever enjoy the company of a man again."

"I've been honest with you about my feelings. And although I also respect your feelings and your need to protect Liam and Donnie, I refuse to be your secret shame."

Daisy's heart sank a bit.

Zeke continued, "That's why it pains me to say this. Take all the time you need. But at this point, I'm going to take a step back. When you're ready to move forward, let me know."

His words pierced her heart. Daisy stared into the dresser mirror for a moment. Her heart palpitated and her stomach roiled. Her chest felt as if it were caving in. She should have anticipated his reaction.

"I understand," she lied.

Who was she kidding? She wanted to explore a relationship with him. She wanted more dinners and walks in the park with him. She wanted to introduce him to Liam and Donnie, and she wanted to meet Esther. But her life was not just about what she wanted. Her sons' relationship was strained. Their sibling bond was fraying under the pressure. Adding stress to her sons' lives was something she would never do deliberately, even if it meant breaking her own heart.

Chapter 14

The drive from Killearn Estates to Whittington Landscape was longer than usual the following day. The traffic light at one of the busiest intersections of Thomasville Road was not working properly. Daisy thought she'd avoid the disaster by taking back roads to the office. The shortcut would get her in the office in time for the meeting with Miss Anderson. Her proactive thinking led her into a major accident upon entering Capital Circle. She sang along with Pandora radio, strategized for the meeting with Miss Anderson, created a grocery list, and even updated her iPhone all to keep her mind off Zeke. Despite her best attempts, Zeke's words played over and over in her head, "Secret shame." She never meant to make him feel that way.

After twenty minutes of waiting in traffic and another five minutes attempting to merge from one lane to the other, Daisy charged through the door of Whittington Landscaping.

"Good morning," said Sophia, looking up from the computer, brows furrowed and mouth tight.

"Good morning."

"I'm glad to see you," said Sophia, voice shaking.

"Is everything all right? I know Liam's anxious. He was uneasy when he left the house this morning. And he called me twice while I was in traffic."

Sophia stammered and looked away. "That's one way of putting it."

"What happened? Was he short with you?"

Meeting Daisy's eyes, Sophia took a deep breath. "No. Nothing like that. Donnie's here."

"Oh! I thought he had another appointment."

"So did Liam."

"Were they arguing?"

Sophia shook her head in confirmation. "It's quiet back there now, but it wasn't earlier. I wasn't brave enough to check on them."

"You shouldn't have to," said Daisy, stepping behind the reception desk. She gently squeezed Sophia's shoulder. "I apologize for their behavior."

"No need to apologize," said Sophia, relaxing slightly. "But I'm really glad you're here."

After offering her an appreciative smile, Daisy glanced at the clock. It was nine thirty-five. She had just a few minutes to chat with Liam and Donnie before Miss Anderson arrived. Like a clear sky morphing into a storm, Daisy's smile faded into a frown when she turned the corner. Her footsteps pounded the floor with the force of her fury, each step echoing through the hallway.

She boomed into the conference room. An unmistakable sense of discord filled the space, marked by the distance between the brothers at opposite ends of the table, their focus exclusively on the papers in front of them.

Daisy closed the door.

Donnie glanced up. "Hi, Mom."

"You made it," said Liam.

She placed her things on the table and stood somewhere between the two of them. "Which one of you is going to tell me what happened in here this morning?"

"What do you mean?" asked Liam.

"We had a little disagreement." Even as a child, Donnie was always the one confessing.

"How do you think your little disagreement sounded to the receptionist? How do you think it made her feel to hear the owners of the business arguing with each other?" She folded her arms across her chest.

"Mrs. Whittington?" Sophia's voice rang over the conference phone.

"Yes?"

"Miss Anderson is here."

"Thank you, Sophia. I'll be right up to escort her back."

"Yes ma'am. I'll let her know."

Daisy removed her things from the table and placed them in an empty chair.

Struggling to keep her voice down, she took in a deep breath to control her anger. "You two better pull it together. Miss Anderson is a long-time client whose account represents twenty-five percent of this company's revenue."

"Exactly! Which is why you should remain seen and not heard." Liam flashed an irritated look at his brother.

Donnie eyed Liam, looking somewhat amused.

Daisy was seconds away from hurting or maiming one or both of her sons. She dropped her arms and turned toward the door, tossing a warning across her shoulder. "Pull it together. You have about half a minute before I bring Miss Anderson into this room. I don't want her to pick up on any of this foolishness."

Stroking the back of his neck, Liam closed his eyes.

Minutes later, Daisy returned to the conference room with Miss Anderson in tow. The petite woman, with more business sites than average, walked with an air of sophistication. She surveyed the surroundings before stopping at the conference table.

Liam and Donnie stood, shaking her hand.

Next, Liam invited her to have a seat. "Thank you for coming. Please feel free to tell us what we've done to displease you."

Miss Anderson sat next to Daisy at the table.

"Like I said on the phone, I'm not happy with the quality of work your company has provided over the last quarter. Unfortunately, if it doesn't improve, I'll have no choice but to find another landscaper."

"Miss Anderson, I assure you we're committed to addressing these issues promptly," said Donnie, his voice laced with concern. "Would you be more specific?"

With a sharp glance, Liam made it clear to his brother that he did not like his question.

Miss Anderson took a deep breath, her eyes drifted to Liam and back to Donnie. "Thank you for asking. I've noticed uneven trimming, poorly maintained flower beds, and weeds."

Liam shook his head as if he had no idea what Miss Anderson was talking about.

She continued. "As you know, I have several buildings around the city, and I consider the condition of the building and the landscaping to be part of my brand."

"Has this been happening all quarter? I'm surprised we're just hearing about this." Liam crossed his arms over his chest, sounding a bit accusatory.

"Regardless of the timing, this issue needs to be addressed," said Miss Anderson, her tone steady and controlled.

"No accusation intended. Your satisfaction is our priority," said Donnie, conveying empathy with his soft tone. "Thank you for letting us know your concerns. We'll take an objective approach in rectifying the situation."

"Yes," said Daisy, clearing her throat. "We will."

"We value your business, and we want to keep that relationship. Are there any other concerns that we can address?" asked Donnie.

"At this point, I can't think of anything else. But please understand that I find this very concerning."

"Thank you," said Donnie. "I'd like to propose a follow-up conversation after each job to ensure our quality of work meets your standards."

Liam glared at Donnie, and Daisy worried an argument might break out. There was no need for a confrontation in front of one of their key clients.

Miss Anderson placed her elbows on the table and steepled her manicured fingers. "That would be great. I'd appreciate that." Her expression morphed from discontent to contentment.

After finalizing a few logistical details, Daisy escorted the newly satisfied customer to the front door.

When Daisy returned, she sat quietly and studied Harold's portrait. After a few moments, she looked at Liam. "Thank you for organizing the meeting."

He nodded, "You're welcome, Mom."

"And you did a great job de-escalating the situation," she said, turning to Donnie.

"No problem." Donnie smiled, but it was more of a sneer. "I'm glad I could help."

"Running a business is not like putting on a show," barked Liam, tightening his jaw.

Daisy took in a deep breath and blew it out slowly. "You know I love both of you, but this bickering has got to stop. I want you to work together to ensure Miss Anderson has everything she needs."

"What do you mean work together?" asked Liam.

"Figure it out! Your father is gone, and I won't be here forever. You'll only have each other. The two of you have been through more than the average siblings go through in a lifetime. Don't let *this*, whatever *this* is, come between you now." She stood, grabbed her things, and walked out the door.

Chapter 15

One week later, the tension between her sons still lingered. She realized Donnie had avoided visiting when he knew Liam was home. Liam stayed out late until he was sure Donnie had left the house. Daisy felt like she was caught in the middle.

Aside from her squabbling sons, Daisy was also dealing with her hurt feelings. She hadn't seen or heard from Zeke for several days. Eight to be exact. Wednesday morning, she busied herself by preparing and submitting invoices for completed projects, following up on outstanding payments, and managing accounts receivables.

It was midmorning when Sophia appeared at her office door with a box from Target Printers.

A huge smile swept across Daisy's face. "They're here!"

"The printer just delivered them." Sophia deposited the box on Daisy's desk.

"These are promotion flyers for Liam's campaign." Daisy took a pair of scissors from the drawer and ripped the box open at the seams.

Sophia stepped aside, waiting patiently.

"They look great!" squealed Daisy, holding up one of the flyers.

Each one bore a close-up shot of Liam's hands holding rich soil with small plants growing in it, representing growth from the ground up. The background faded into a vibrant landscape. The words "From Roots to Results-Vote Liam Whittington" sat below the image in big, bold letters.

"They turned out better than I expected. I plan to distribute them to local businesses, community centers, and other high-traffic areas."

"I can post them on the company's social media and the webpage," said Sophia. "And I'll pass some out to my friends and family."

"That's a wonderful idea. Thank you."

"I think I'll grab Rosie and drag her to Working Class Wednesday tonight. There'll be plenty of business owners at the event. It'll be fun."

After a few minutes of brainstorming campaign ideas together, Sophia left Daisy's office. Daisy paused before getting back to work. Thoughts of Zeke filled her head. She missed their daily calls and texts. He promised to help with Liam's campaign. She wondered if his offer still stood. He'd made it clear he was taking a step back from the relationship. There was only one way to find out.

She tapped his number into the cell phone and waited for an answer.

"Hello." His deep baritone voice was music to her soul.

"Hi. It's Daisy," she whispered, bracing for a negative response.

"How are you?" If Zeke was happy to hear from her, she couldn't tell.

"Fine. I wasn't sure if you were still interested in helping with Liam's campaign," she hurried her words. "We just received the flyers and posters. If you don't want to help, I understand."

He was silent for a moment. Butterflies fluttered around her stomach. What had she done? Zeke didn't want to hear from her, and he didn't want to spend time with her passing out flyers. He just couldn't find the words to tell her. At least that's what she believed.

"Yes, I can pick them up from your receptionist."

Daisy didn't have a good feeling about him coming to the office. Liam would have questions. "I can bring them to you. I don't mind."

An awkward pause followed before Zeke spoke. "You're afraid I'll run into your son, aren't you?"

"No, that's not it," she lied. "You're doing me a favor, and I want to save you the trouble of coming all the way out to the office."

"Then you haven't talked to your sons about me?" Obviously, he wasn't buying her excuse.

Daisy rolled her eyes; grateful he couldn't see through the phone. "No. Not yet."

"I see. You can drop them off at your convenience. I'll be glad to help," he said.

Another awkward silence ensued.

Finally, he asked, "Is there anything else?"

"No. Thanks again for your help."

"Sure. If there's nothing else. I should get back to work."

"I understand. I'll be there shortly." Daisy ended the call, leaning back against her chair. One more irritated man in her life.

From the sound of his voice, Zeke wanted nothing to do with her. Maybe she could convince him to change his mind when she delivered the flyers to his office.

***

"I think it would be best if I wait until after the awards ceremony to tell Liam and Donnie about us. Why don't we continue to see each other privately until then? Can you find it in your heart to do that?"

Daisy practiced the words she wanted to say to Zeke over and over until she arrived at the Elegance Event Center. Unlike the night of Liam and Lorraine's engagement party, only a few vehicles sprinkled the lot. None of the cars were familiar. Daisy assumed Zeke's truck was in the rear of the building. After a quick prayer, asking God to soften Zeke's heart, she reached for a bag of flyers and moved toward the entrance.

Upon arriving at the front entrance, Daisy was surprised to find it locked. She knocked and a young woman dressed in a pair of jeans, a colorful t-shirt, and flip-flops appeared from one of the offices. The twenty-something-year-old inspected Daisy before walking toward her. A glimmer of recognition pulled at Daisy's memory as she tried to place the young female. After fidgeting with the keys for a few moments, the woman unlocked the door and stepped aside so Daisy could enter.

"You must be Daisy Whittington?"

"Yes, I am."

"I'm Esther Daniel. It's nice to finally meet you."

"Esther? You're …"

"Zeke's daughter. My dad isn't here. He asked me to meet you. Said you wanted to drop off some flyers."

"Yes," said Daisy, attempting to hide her disappointment. Zeke knew she was coming. She handed the flyers to Esther, avoiding eye contact.

"Do you have a few minutes to chat?" asked Esther.

"Yes, I do." Daisy tried to appear calm despite her nerves.

"Great. Let's sit in the lobby." Daisy followed Esther into the lobby. She sat on one end of the sofa, and Esther sat on the other.

"Dad says your son has been nominated for Entrepreneur of the Year. Congratulations to him and you."

"Thank you." Daisy looked down the hall, remembering the time spent with Zeke.

"You're welcome. I guess you're wondering what this is all about?"

"I can probably guess. If you're anything like my sons, you want to talk about my involvement with your father."

"Correct," Esther said, dryly. "But unlike your sons, my father respected me enough to tell me about you."

"I don't think you understand …"

"Perhaps you are the one who doesn't understand," she said, leaning forward. "I love my father. He was hurt deeply after my mother died. Not only did he lose his wife, but he also discovered that his entire marriage had been a lie."

"I didn't know that." Daisy's lips puckered as she drew in a sharp breath.

"Did he tell you that my mother's boyfriend was driving her car at the time of the accident?"

Daisy's eyes widened. "No, he didn't."

"Mom was supposed to be going out of town on business. Instead, she and her boyfriend were planning a secret rendezvous. Can you imagine the shame and embarrassment my father felt, all while dealing with the death of the love of his life?"

"I'm so sorry."

"He tried to get past it. He did fine for a while. Even dated a few women, here and there. Nothing serious, just companionship. He was careful to guard his heart. But the town was just too small, and there were too many memories. So, when Mr. Arthur offered Dad a chance to start over in a new city, he went for it."

Esther hesitated for a moment, before continuing.

"When they bought this building, I wasn't sure about it. It was a mess. But Mr. Arthur and Dad saw something I didn't see. And I'm glad they did. Look at it now. It's beautiful and it's a thriving business. I was happy for them, especially for Dad. He deserved a little happiness. Then something changed. He seemed almost blissful, he smiled more and sang more. He was cheerier than I'd seen him in a long time. Then one day, he called to tell me about you."

Daisy released a guilty smile.

"Dad went through a deeply personal and challenging journey to get to the point where he could open his heart to another woman."

"I understand."

"If you do, then you also understand why he has set healthy boundaries to protect himself."

Daisy tried to pull it together. The last thing she wanted to do was fall apart in front of Zeke's daughter. "Yes, I do."

"If you do, then you need to decide. Either tell your sons how you feel about my father or stay away from him. No more calls or texts. No more excuses to visit. Please don't cause him any more pain than he's already experienced. He deserves to be happy."

"You're right. He does," Daisy said, trying to remain composed. "I understand your concerns, and I appreciate how much you love and care for your father. This is difficult for all of us. I want you to know I genuinely care for Zeke, and his happiness means a lot to me. I never meant to hurt him."

"I'm glad we understand each other," said Esther, matter-of-factly. Then she stood. "I'll make sure Dad gets these flyers."

Daisy also stood, feeling as if she was being dismissed from the principal's office. "Thank you. I'll see myself out."

Daisy's feet couldn't move fast enough. Dignity draining, she hastened to the door. Hurting Zeke was never her goal. Neither was hurting her sons. How could she balance her happiness with the fears and concerns of the people she cared about?

Once inside her car, her eyes welled with tears. First, a single drop escaped, descending gradually down her cheek. She blinked, trying to hold back the tidal wave of emotions. Then another tear dropped, and another and another, each one faster than the other.

***

Daisy and Rosie entered Cascades Park for Working Class Wednesday's networking event that evening. A whiff of grilled onions and savory bell peppers drifted from the air and made its way to Daisy's nose.

"That smells incredible!" said Rosie. "I hope Mack's Kitchen is vending today. I could go for one of those sausage dogs."

"Can you wait until we pass out a few flyers?"

"Of course. I can get a couple on the way out because I want to take one home to Donzel. He loves them."

Daisy adjusted her tote bag strap and glanced around. Donned in a mix of professional and casual attire, people mingled in various-sized groups. Some exchanged business cards, others engaged in conversations. Some wore nametags, others wore lanyards, and some wore clothing identifying themselves. Booths and tables with company banners and promotional materials scattered along the sidewalks. Despite the lively setting, Daisy couldn't shake her frustration.

The last time she attended this event was with Zeke. It was a couple of hours of fun, laughter, and getting to know one another. By the end of the evening, it was evident they enjoyed each other's company. And that scared her. If only she could have gotten over the fear of telling her boys about him.

This evening's not about you. It's about Liam and his nomination for Entrepreneur of the Year. So, get it together and brag about your son.

"Wow!" said Rosie, looking around the park, "There are a lot of people here. Where should we begin?"

Daisy looked around the grounds. The event began about thirty minutes earlier and participants already filled the venue.

"How about we start at the first vendor table and work our way around. We can also give a flyer to anyone in attendance."

"That'll work."

Daisy handed Rosie a stack of flyers as they moved forward, she noticed a familiar face.

"Daisy! It's good to see you," called out David Wheeler, the owner of The Power Equipment Shop, and long-time friend of the family.

"Hi, David," Daisy replied with a forced smile, walking over to his vendor table. "How are you? Do you have a moment? I'd like to talk to you about something."

"Of course." David turned to his helper, "Would you mind taking over until I return?"

Daisy took a few steps away from the table, pulling out a flyer from her bag.

"Liam's been nominated for this award," she began, her voice slightly unsteady. "He's worked so hard. I think he deserves to win. And it's not because I'm his mother. I'd appreciate it if you would vote for him and maybe urge your customers to do the same."

David studied the flyer. "Liam's a great kid. I've watched him grow and flourish, especially as a businessman. I'd be happy to vote for him."

"Thank you, David."

They chatted for a few minutes, but Daisy couldn't help but think about Zeke. He would have been with her, supporting her with this campaign, offering words of encouragement. But he wasn't. He'd stepped away, leaving a void she was struggling to fill. Zeke wanted more from their relationship. He wanted openness, honesty, and a place in her life she wasn't ready to give him. Not yet.

"How's everything else going?" David's question pulled Daisy from her thoughts.

"Things are pretty good. Thanks. I should let you get back to your table."

"May I have a few of those flyers? I'll post them around the shop."

"Oh, that would be great. Thanks."

Daisy handed David a handful of flyers and moved on to the next table. As she moved from vendor to vendor, making her pitch, Daisy's smile grew strained.

"Is everything all right?" asked Alice, better known as the *Paparazzi* lady, when Daisy arrived at her table.

"I'm fine. Got a lot going on," she admitted, handing her a flyer. "Liam's been nominated for an award. I'm campaigning for him."

"Now, that's a mother's love. We'll do anything for our children, won't we?" Alice took the flyers. "You and your family have always done right by this community. He has my vote."

"Thank you," Daisy said softly.

She turned, practically colliding with Rosie.

"All gone," announced Rosie, with palms upward and shoulders shrugged.

"You're done?"

"Yes, ma'am."

"Thank you so much. Now let's head to the food vendors." Daisy walked down the sidewalk with her friend, chatting along the way. They'd spent a lot of time together over the years, and Daisy appreciated the companionship.

"What's up with you and Zeke?" asked Rosie, pointing to the numerous food vendors on the hill.

"There is no Zeke and me," said Daisy trying to figure out how she was going to relay the latest developments. "You know what I mean."

Daisy told Rosie about arranging to bring flyers to Zeke, and how he asked his daughter to be there to retrieve the flyers.

"You're kidding me. Have you met her before?"

"No. But Zeke talked about her often. It was easy to see how much she cares about her father."

"As it should be."

"Esther was straightforward and to the point. I knew immediately she didn't care for me at all."

"I'm sorry that happened to you. What are you going to do?"

"I'm going to stay as far away from Zeke as possible. After everything he went through with his wife, he deserves to have an open and honest relationship with a woman. And that's something I can't give him."

"You can't or you won't?"

"I won't"

Rosie didn't say anything.

As they waited in the food line, all Daisy could do was hope that one day Zeke would understand.

Chapter 16

Daisy rose early the next morning. Sitting at the kitchen table reading Scripture on her iPad, she struggled to understand how Psalms 30:11 pertained to her, "Thou hast turned for me my mourning into dancing: thou hast put off my sackcloth and girded me with gladness."

It'd been a long sleepless night with thoughts of Zeke filling her head.

Some people lived their entire lives searching for someone to share it with, Harold and she had found each other early in life. They invited Christ into the marriage and did their best to please Him. God blessed them with two loving sons by way of adoption. The favor of God seemed to be on their union as their love prospered. Then one evening as they enjoyed dinner, Harold complained of chest pains. Emergency services were called, they rushed him to the hospital, and just like that, he was gone.

It took Daisy a while to bounce back. But she did—content to live the remainder of her days alone.

Then out of nowhere, Zeke entered her life. It felt good to meet someone who understood the pain of losing a spouse. He understood loneliness and the guilt and shame of wanting to try again. She fought hard to keep the walls around her heart, but somehow, Zeke got through. But he wanted her to do the one thing she couldn't. She could not and would not hurt her sons by bringing another man into their lives. Zeke backed away, unwilling to be her "secret shame" as he called it. Now, his daughter wanted Daisy to respect his wishes and do the same.

"Good morning. You're up early," Liam said, entering the kitchen. He placed a kiss on her cheek.

"Yes, I am. Couldn't sleep so I decided to get a little Bible study in."

"I don't want to disturb you." Liam leaned against the kitchen counter.

"You're not. I was just re-reading a few things. I'm done." Daisy swiped up on the iPad screen and the Scriptures disappeared. "How are you?"

"Good." Liam slipped into the seat next to his mother. "I'm meeting Lorraine at Starbucks in a few. She asked me to bring some flyers with me. She's going to post them on the billboards in her office building. I really wish you guys would tone it down some. I agreed to accept the nomination, but I'm not comfortable with this promoting stuff."

"Umm-hmm," said Daisy. "The other two nominees are advocating for themselves, why shouldn't you? I heard an ad for one of them on the gospel radio station yesterday. Besides you're not promoting yourself, we are."

"I suppose," Liam grumbled. "But you and Lorraine are doing too much."

"Hush now. We can't help it if we love and adore you, and we think you deserve to be Tallahassee's Entrepreneur of the Year."

"I know, Mom. I'm grateful for your love and support. And as far as Lorraine goes, I can't wait to marry her. If I had it my way, we'd be married already."

Daisy reached for his hand. "Be patient and let her have the wedding of her dreams."

"Patient? I think I've been. Look how long it took me to find her. That's because I want what you and Dad had. That was special and that's what I want for Lorraine and me. That's Lorraine," he said, glancing at his pinging phone. "She texted me a reminder to bring the flyers. I guess I should get dressed. I'll see you at the office, Mom."

"Hey, why don't you invite Lorraine to dinner after church on Sunday? I'll make that tetrazzini dish she enjoyed last time."

"I'm sure she'd like that. Oh, and just so you know, I'm going to Donnie's place after I meet Lorraine."

Daisy looked up, waiting to hear more.

"We're going to ride together to each of Miss Anderson's sites. After we assess the situation, we'll discuss a plan to move forward."

Daisy considered his words. They planned to work together. She didn't want to seem too zealous, although she was. "That's great."

"I'm not making any promises," said Liam. "But it's a step in the right direction."

Daisy chuckled. "Weeds."

"Excuse me?" he asked.

"Weeds. Miss Anderson mentioned weeds. They're pesky little plants that grow with the flowers. They steal nutrients, occupy space, and pilfer water."

Liam sighed. "Yes, I know. We'll be sure to pull the weeds."

"But they have a purpose," Daisy continued. "Weed roots can break up soil and unearth nutrients from below ground. Dead weeds decompose into humus. And you know what happens then?"

"Botany 101." Liam nodded. One side of his mouth raised slightly in a smile. "The humus increases the soil's moisture and nutrient retention."

"That's right. Weeds are growing in the relationship between your brother and you. Find the weeds and kill them. Then watch something wonderful happen."

***

Daisy pulled into the parking spot in front of Whittington Landscaping and uttered a quick prayer for her sons. "Dear

Heavenly Father, I realize Liam and Donnie are a gift from You and I thank You. Please forgive me if I've done anything to lead them away from You. Father, I pray that despite their disagreements, they'll endeavor to love and overcome this conflict. Your Word says in Romans eight verse twenty-eight that all things work together for good to them that love God, to them who are the called according to *His* purpose. And I believe that something good will come from their disagreement. In Christ's name, I pray. Amen."

Like a balloon slowly deflating, she let out a deep breath, releasing her tension into the air. Grateful for the privilege of prayer, she gathered her purse and exited the car. She'd learned from experience that when she prayed about a matter, there was no need to worry. But she also knew the practice was easier said than done.

***

Daisy entered the office with a smile. "Good morning, Sophia."

"Hello, Mrs. Whittington."

"I'm going to conduct a budget review today. Please hold all my calls."

"Yes, ma'am."

One of her responsibilities was to maintain control over the company's finances to ensure the business remained profitable and sustainable. If Miss Anderson decided to take her business elsewhere, they'd better have a plan to sustain the loss and identify areas for adjustments.

With a few clicks on the computer, she pulled the previous month's budget, recent financial statements, recent invoices, and receipts up on the screen. Daisy spent most of the morning entering numbers and adjusting formulas, her head began to ache from all the calculating. Her hard work paid off because she found three immediate ways to cut costs and several ways to increase cash flow. The solutions were short-term but effective, and she looked forward to sharing them with her sons.

After finishing the budget, Daisy turned her attention to work on anything that would keep her mind from thinking about Zeke. She missed his surprise texts during the day and his late-night phone calls. She longed to hear his stories about life in the Marine Corps and his travels overseas. She even missed the way he jiggled his keys in his pants pocket.

A tap on her door pulled her out of her musing.

"Why does planning a wedding have to be so difficult?" asked Liam,

Daisy laughed. "What are you talking about? Lorraine is doing most of the hard work."

"That's true, but I don't like the endless decision-making. Who cares what color the napkins are? And what difference does it make if we have roses or peonies? What about the tedious details like seating arrangements?" He flailed one hand then the other.

Daisy leaned, hoping to discern whether he wanted a listening ear or motherly advice.

"I just want to get married. Why should I care about that other stuff?" he asked.

"Because Lorraine cares about all of those things," said Daisy. "When your father acted like he didn't care about the things that were important to me, it hurt my feelings."

Liam looked dissatisfied for a moment, and then he squared his shoulders and said, "I don't want Lorraine to feel that way. Thanks for sharing that. What's going on around here?"

"Not much. I spent most of the morning working on ways to cut costs and increase cash flow in case Miss Anderson decides to pull her account. I have a few ideas I'd like to share. But first, how did things go with Donnie and you this morning?"

"Fine. We went to the worksite. Miss Anderson was right. The work was sloppy."

"What do the two of you plan to do to correct it and ensure it doesn't happen again?"

"I don't need Donnie for those things. I've been in the business a long time, and I know how to deal with dissatisfied customers."

Daisy looked across the desk at the heartfelt portrait of her boys, now men, side-by-side. Their personalities shone through in every smile and glance, a perfect reflection of their journey together. They'd worked together to plan the photo shoot and to surprise her with prints. It was the perfect present.

She pulled her eyes away from the picture and looked at Liam again.

"This is not just about solving the problem. It's about working with your brother to solve the problem."

"Okay, Mom. I get it. We'll work on this together."

Daisy placed her hands in her lap. "Umm-hmm."

"Just so you know, this afternoon, I'm meeting with the crew responsible for the work and other key team members to discuss what went wrong. I'll determine whether it's a training issue, a communication breakdown, or just poor workmanship."

"I see that MBA is working," she teased.

Liam chuckled. "Then I'll develop a set of clear, measurable standards for future projects, ensuring that the team knows what's expected of them to avoid similar problems."

"That's a great start." Daisy leaned forward in her chair, resting her elbows on the desk. Her eyes flitted to Liam with a mixture of eagerness and resolve.

She gestured energetically with her hands as she continued. "Donnie has all these theatrical skills—think about what he could do if we gave him more room to shine in the business. I don't know, maybe he could create a hands-on training experience for the employees? Perhaps design role-playing scenarios where workers practice dealing with customer complaints and performing high-quality work under pressure. His approach can make training more engaging and memorable."

Her countenance shifted to a curious squint as she assessed Liam's expression. Then she leaned back and laced her fingers together in front of her as a confident smile extended across her face. "What do you think?"

Liam didn't answer right away. Daisy could tell from the way his lips pressed into a firm line that he was fighting against the hint of a smile. He liked the idea but didn't want her to know it.

She continued, "Donnie could create visual aids or even videos that illustrate proper landscaping techniques, and what a "good job" looks like. We could use the training materials to ensure the crew understands and can replicate our standards across all sites."

Liam tilted his head slowly, almost inattentively, as if he were contemplating her words with promising approval. "Perhaps," he said.

Daisy was disappointed that working together had not led her sons to a better understanding of each other. But she wasn't ready to give up. If she continued to force the issue, perhaps it would lead to a stronger bond in the long run or further intervention from her could lead to one or both sons feeling manipulated, leading to further emotional distance.

Something had to change, and she was determined to make it happen.

Chapter 17

On Sunday morning, Daisy lost herself in praise and worship. Not even Sister Rosalind Jefferson's overindulgent use of White Diamonds perfume could distract her. She drenched herself in the fragrance every Sunday, and anyone who sat two rows in front or behind her was sure to get a nose full. On more than one occasion, Rosie threatened to confront Rosalind when the scent triggered an allergic reaction, sending her into a sneezing fit.

Today, Daisy focused on the goodness of God. She entered the sanctuary feeling sorry for herself. She forced those thoughts aside and replaced them with thoughts of adoration for the Heavenly Father. Then Pastor Johnson preached on 1 Chronicles 16 34, "O give thanks unto the LORD; for *He is* good; for His mercy *endureth* forever." She couldn't focus on God and her problems simultaneously.

After service, Daisy said goodbye to a few people. Then she walked outside and stood on the porch.

"Daisy Whittington, I know you aren't leaving without saying goodbye or see you later."

Daisy continued down the stairs and then turned to face her friend.

"I'm sorry. I've got a lot on my mind. Lorraine's coming over for dinner. I have a few things to do before she arrives."

Rosie drew her eyebrows together and hesitated before speaking. "I have something to tell you."

"Tell me later. I gotta go." Daisy motioned to leave.

"No," Rosie trotted down the steps, taking a deep breath. "I need to tell you now."

Her quivering voice stopped Daisy in her tracks.

"What is it?"

Rosie's lips pressed into a thin line, eyes flashing an I-hate-to-be-the-one-to-tell-you look. "I saw Irma Jones and Zeke at the farmer's market yesterday. They looked cozy. She had her hands all over him. Now you know how she is. I don't know if she was marking her territory or what. It doesn't take much with her. Throw that dog a bone, and she goes right after it."

Daisy was so shocked she could hardly breathe. "Oh, really," she mumbled, pretending it didn't matter.

"Maybe it wasn't what it looked like," Rosie offered a brief, sad smile.

"Zeke is free to date whomever he chooses." Attempting to appear nonchalant and relaxed, Daisy groped her purse.

"It won't take long for him to realize she's a–."

"Rosie! You're still on the church grounds. Watch your mouth."

"You know I'm telling the truth. Mary Magdalene wasn't the only woman of ill repute."

"Shame on you. Listen, I gotta go. I have a lot to do. Zeke and I weren't meant to be."

"How do you know that?"

"God blessed me with love once. I can't ask Him to do it again."

Raising her eyebrows, Rosie leaned forward. "Oh *reeeally*? So, you're saying God is like Best Buy?"

Daisy rolled her eyes. "What are you talking about?"

"You know how on Black Friday after Christmas when they put the flat screen TVs on sale? One per customer … Are you saying God has only one love per saint?"

"I don't have time for your foolishness. I need to get home." Daisy wiggled her fingers in the air and stomped to her car.

Zeke and Irma. An image of the two of them together played over and over in her mind as she drove the distance from church to home. Her heart pounded. He'd wanted an open and honest relationship, and now he'd moved on.

She struggled to make sense of it all. She'd finally learned to manage life without Harold and open her heart to someone new; yet she couldn't find the courage to take the next step forward. Would she spend the rest of her life alone?

So what if Zeke and Irma were at the Farmers Market together? Maybe they arrived separately and ran into each other there. No matter how they got there, they were together. It looks like I discarded Zeke, and he ran right into the arms of another woman.

Arriving home, Daisy donned an apron and went to work. Forty-five minutes later, the vegetables were chopped, the roux was done, and the andouille sausage was browned. That's when Liam entered with Lorraine by his side.

"Smells good in here," he said, carrying a large covered serving dish.

"Hey, you two. Come on in."

"I know we're a little early, but Lorraine insisted on helping you prepare dinner."

"Yes, I did." Lorraine shrugged. "Besides, it's a good way for me to learn how to make gumbo. Liam says it's one of his favorites. I made banana pudding for dessert. It's the least I could do."

"Thank you. You're a sweetheart," Daisy said, once again impressed by Lorraine's thoughtfulness. She was glad Lorraine was by Liam's side.

Liam placed the pudding in the refrigerator.

"I'm almost done here." Daisy added broth, vegetables, and roux to the pot. "All I have left to do is add a little okra, chicken, and sausage. The shrimp is in the fridge. I'll add them to the pot later."

"How can I help?" asked Lorraine, washing her hands at the sink.

"Yeah, how can I help?" teased Liam.

"Make yourself scarce, son. Lorraine and I can handle this. Donnie will be here soon; I don't want any shenanigans out of the two of you."

"Just remember, if there's trouble, he started it," teased Liam, disappearing into the other room.

The women worked together to finish cooking. Daisy shared a few of her secret ingredients with Lorraine. While the rice cooked, Lorraine set the table. Daisy was busy adding the final ingredients to the gumbo when Donnie entered through the garage.

"Is it time to eat?" he asked. "I'm hungry."

"Almost," said Daisy, stirring the pot of gumbo.

Donnie walked over to the stove and wrapped his arms around his mother. "Hey, Mom." Then he turned to Lorraine, "Hey, Lorraine. It's always nice to see you."

Liam emerged from the other room. "Little brother, what'd I tell you about flirting with my fiancé?" he teased and shooed Donnie away.

"I'm just speaking the truth. I'm always happy to see her beautiful face. Still can't figure out what she sees in you, though."

Daisy gave the gumbo one last stir. "Go wash up, you two. It's time to eat."

When her sons disappeared, Daisy set out a fresh vegetable salad she'd made earlier.

"Would you find a serving dish for the rice?" she asked Lorraine. "And I'll do the same for the cornbread and the gumbo."

When everyone was seated, Liam blessed the food, and they dug in.

"You must be special," Donnie said to Lorraine. "Usually, Mom leaves all the food on the stove, and we have to fend for ourselves."

Lorraine leaned her head to the side and raised an eyebrow. "Thank you, Mrs. Whittington. But you didn't have to go through all that trouble."

"No trouble at all. I wanted to do it. Besides, it's been a while since we all broke bread together. I miss this," said Daisy with a wave of her hand.

Donnie scooped a spoonful of gumbo. "We ate dinner together all the time when we were kids."

Daisy glanced at her sons; the memory brought a smile to her face.

"Liam, did you share my idea about company training with your brother?"

"No. I don't think he will be interested."

"What's the idea?" Donnie looked around the table before settling his eyes on his mother.

Daisy shared her idea with Donnie and Lorraine.

"I'd love to be involved like that." He smiled.

Donnie turned to Liam whose scowl preceded the impending anxiety to the table. "But I'm not surprised you didn't share it with me. Just your way of monopolizing Dad's legacy."

Donnie's antagonistic words were like a whirlwind sucking all the pleasure out of the room. Lorraine fidgeted in her seat. Daisy could tell she was embarrassed.

Liam ground his teeth and flexed his muscles. "Well, if you hadn't abandoned us and gone chasing the life of a thespian, maybe I could trust you with some responsibility."

Donnie huffed. "I haven't abandoned the family. Weren't you the one who encouraged me to follow my dreams? Don't be a hypocrite. You can't have it both ways."

Liam glanced at Lorraine. "Honey, you're going to be a part of this family. You may as well see what you're getting into."

"Can't we at least have a decent dinner? You two can argue later." Daisy eyed her sons. The only thing that stopped her from yelling was the fact that she didn't want to embarrass Lorraine any further.

Whack! Whack! Whack!

Liam slammed his fist on the table so hard, it made the glasses dance.

How dare he throw a temper tantrum like a two-year-old. Liam was a grown man getting ready to take on the responsibilities of a husband, and here he is behaving like a child.

Outraged, Daisy turned to him, ready to issue a reprimand.

What she saw made her heart skip a beat!

Chapter 18

Daisy's eyes fell upon Liam and stayed there. She watched him grab his chest and gasped for air. Her body froze in fear. To say what Daisy experienced was déjà vu would be an understatement. It was at this very table years earlier that she watched Harold grasp his chest in pain, the onset of his fatal heart attack.

Lorraine jolted to her feet and clutched her chest. "Liam, are you okay?"

His only response was to grasp his neck.

Donnie cocked his head on an angle and raised an eyebrow. "He's choking!" He jumped from his seat and rushed to help.

"I think you're right!"

The mood shifted to sheer panic and dread. The room fell silent except for the sound of gasps and hearts racing.

Donnie leaned Liam forward. He struck several sharp blows to his back between the shoulder blades. Nothing worked.

Lorraine reached for her phone, ready to dial 9-1-1.

Too frightened to move, Daisy watched Donnie position himself behind Liam, make a fist, and place it just above his brother's navel. Then he grabbed the fist with his other hand and pushed it several times.

After a few strong thrusts, a piece of sausage flew out of Liam's mouth and onto the table.

With his airways free, Liam released a few coughs. Everyone else released a sigh of relief.

"Thanks, bro," said Liam, hoarsely, with a weak smile.

"Thank you, Jesus," whispered Daisy with her hands lifted.

Lorraine removed a glass of water from the side of Liam's bowl and offered it to him.

Donnie's quick action saved his brother, but the room was frozen in stunned silence. It felt as if time stopped, the air thick with disbelief.

Lorraine returned to her seat, shut her eyes for a moment and released a steady stream of air. "It's okay. We're all okay."

"I'm so glad you were here, Lorraine. Thank you." Daisy walked over to Liam, leaning in for a hug.

"I'm okay." Liam glanced from Daisy to Donnie and back.

Daisy returned to her chair. She exchanged a wide-eyed look with Liam and then Donnie. Her breaths shallow, as the haunting echo of Harold's collapse years ago rippled through the room. Even though the crisis had passed, they sat there as if in a dream.

Shadows of the past felt much too close.

"Lorraine," said Liam, taking another sip of water. "I suppose I should explain something to you."

Lorraine glanced around the table. "I sense it has something to do with your father."

"Years ago, we were sitting down at dinner, when Dad suddenly grabbed his chest in pain." Liam pushed his plate toward the center of the table. "He broke out in a sweat and started gasping for air. We were scared."

Daisy jumped in, "Harold had always been the one in control. It was difficult to watch him become helpless."

"We were all helpless," added Donnie. "We called 9-1-1. Dad died at the hospital a few hours later."

"Thank you, guys, for sharing that with me. I know I was scared watching my Liam in distress. But the three of you were re-experiencing an incredibly heartbreaking memory," said Lorraine. "Thank God, Liam is fine, and we're all here together. From what I've learned about Mr. Whittington, I think he wouldn't want you all to dwell on how he died. In fact, I would even venture to say, he had hopes and dreams for the future for all of you.”

Daisy smiled. “You’re right. He wanted his sons to live happy and fulfilled lives.”

She turned to Liam, “He knew you wanted to work in the business. That’s why he took the time to teach you everything he knew. And you,” she continued, turning to Donnie. “He knew you loved the theatre, and he planned for you to fulfill your dream also.”

“Mom …” Donnie attempted to interrupt.

“Let me finish,” she said, in a low voice with one hand raised in a calming gesture. “I wonder how proud he would be knowing that you two found a way to fulfill your dreams while working together? I just believe he would be happier than an aphid on a budding flower.”

“And what about you, Mrs. Whittington? What did he want for your future?”

“Believe it or not, we talked about what would happen if one of us should die,” said Daisy.

“You did?” asked Liam.

“On several occasions. He wanted me to be happy, too. He wanted me to find love again.”

Daisy looked around the table. All eyes were on her. Embarrassed, she said, “I haven’t been able to bring myself to even think about love again. Enough about the past. Let’s eat before dinner gets cold.”

“Okay,” said Donnie, turning to his brother. “But this time, can you chew your food before you swallow it?”

Everyone laughed.

It was just like Donnie to bring laughter to an otherwise awkward moment. But just as quickly as the laughter penetrated the atmosphere, it faded. And they were left to their thoughts in the still, pensive dining room.

***

Liam sat and scanned the concerned faces of his loved ones around the table, his chest still stiff from panic. His eyes traveled to his mother first. Daisy sat trembling with her hands clutched together as if in prayer. Her usual composed source of strength was now replaced with her shaking presence. She didn't speak, but her glistening wide eyes expressed all the words she couldn't find.

He shifted to Lorraine next. Her beautiful eyes pierced right through him, holding a combination of concern and relief. Her gaze, typically heartfelt and warm, was now rigid and intense as if to confirm he was still there. Her hand sat on the edge of the table, quivering slightly, her fingers stroked the surface in an unconscious tempo.

Finally, his eyes landed on Donnie. Broad-shouldered and fit, his brother looked as though he was calm, arms crossed over his chest. But Liam wasn't fooled. Beneath Donnie's brave facade, his jaw was taut, and his eyes darted to Liam every few seconds as if confirming whether he was okay.

The dining room, permeating with the scent of their interrupted meal, felt heavier now. Cutting through the tense silence, the purr of the ceiling fan overhead seemed unusually loud. Liam took in a slow deep breath, his gaze looped back to his mother, his fiancée, and his brother—three people whose love and devotion now felt like a protective shield around him.

***

Later that evening, Liam walked Lorraine to her car and stepped into his father's office. Laughter drifted from the living room, where Daisy and Donnie watched an episode of "America's Funniest Videos." He'd declined the invitation to join them. Memories sprung up like wildflowers—beautiful but entangled with prickly regrets and crawling vines of unanswered questions. The room, though still, flourished with echoes of times past, a landscape Liam wasn't sure how to navigate.

A snapshot of a life paused midmotion. Harold Whittington's home office stood behind French doors. A modest oak desk remained the room's centerpiece, flanked by bookshelves extended along one wall. The shelves were lined with books on business and landscaping. A well-worn Bible seemed to anchor the space. His favorite old recliner, sat in the corner, scuffed at the arms but still exuding comfort.

Family pictures peppered the walls and shelves, their jovial faces frozen in time. The desk held little clutter. Just enough to indicate someone had once worked there with intention. Amid the objects was a coffee mug, its presence a quiet memento of mornings spent in deep thought or prayer.

Though the room was seldom used, it remained cared for, with a layer of polish holding dust at bay, thanks to Daisy's occasional visits. Yet, the room possessed a solemn stillness, a place where time seemed unwilling to move forward.

Liam fell into the recliner with a quiet thump, the cushions giving a recognizable sigh beneath him.

When he was a child, Liam spent hours in the old recliner talking with his father. It was where he learned a multitude of life lessons.

"Put God first in all you do.
Work hard and pay your bills on time.
Always be good to your mother.
Have your brother's back.
One day, it will be just the two of you, and the relationship you have will be the one you created years earlier..."

The phone rang, yanking Liam out of his thoughts. A smile spread across his face at Lorraine's image on the screen.

"Hello, beautiful."

"Are you resting?"

Liam reached down to the right, his fingers finding the cold metal lever by instinct. He pulled it up and the footrest snatched forward. "Actually, I'm sitting in Dad's office. How are your parents?"

"They're fine."

"I thought about bringing some work in here." He leaned back, sank in deeper, the chair creaking around him.

"I think you should take it easy. Dinner was a whirlwind of emotions, and we all need a break. Anyway, I'm chatting with my parents about wedding plans, then I'm headed home to rest."

"Enjoy your time with your parents. Don't worry about me. I love you. Call me when you get home."

After disconnecting the call, Liam's thoughts returned to his father. He walked over to the shelf, running his hand along a row of books. Then he sat in the desk chair gazing at the family pictures. His eyes fell on the photo of the framed first dollar made after Whittington Landscaping received its business license.

Curiosity drew him to the lower left drawer, where wills and trust papers, financial records, and life insurance policies were meticulously organized and labeled. Harold Whittington ensured everything was in order in the event of his death. Liam planned to do the same.

Thumbing through the files, Liam came across an unlabeled manilla folder sealed with a broken clasp. A well-worn flap indicated his father frequented the contents. Funny he hadn't noticed it before. Would it be intrusive to peek inside? On more than one occasion, his mother encouraged Liam and his brother to search the items in the office, if only to learn more about their father. Heeding his mother's words, Liam opened the envelope and emptied its contents on the desk.

Photos of Liam and Donnie as children with handwritten notes on the back, old report cards, art projects, and awards from their school years were among the contents. Liam paused when he found a playbill from one of Donnie's theater performances, with his father's handwritten notes in the margin. "Donnie stole the show!" and "So proud of him."

Liam leaned back in the chair and reflected.

Even as a child, Donnie would spontaneously act out scenes from their favorite shows. He'd capture our attention around the dinner table, sharing stories with dramatic flair.

During his freshman year, Donnie's interest turned into passion, earning him the lead role in the school's production of "The Wiz." Dad was so proud; he invited everyone from work and church to see the production. He was sure Donnie would do great.

And he was right. It was more than just a school play. It was a segway to many other high school and community performances. Dad attended every one of Donnie's shows until the day he died.

Dad supported Donnie's passion then, and I'm sure he would support him now, especially when Donnie is at the pinnacle of graduating. Who knows what opportunities await? Maybe I've been looking at things the wrong way. If Dad could support him all those years ago, maybe I should reevaluate my stance.

Chapter 19

A mixture of compact cars, older vehicles, and a few luxury cars packed every lot on the FAMU campus Monday morning. Bike racks filled with bicycles, and a few electric scooters scattered the building entrances. Liam circled the parking lot once more, wondering why he thought it was a good idea to drop in on Donnie's rehearsal in the first place.

After a reflective evening in his father's office the night before, he'd reconsidered his attitude toward Donnie. Perhaps his theatre skills could be put to good use. Donnie mentioned something about having practice Monday morning. He'd seen his brother acting on stage many times. But something drew Liam to the campus to see what went on before the curtains were opened to the audience.

Liam pulled into an empty spot not far from the theatre. He stepped out of the car to feed the meter. Students, laden with backpacks and earbuds, rushed to class. Groups of friends chatted near their cars or by building entrances. Two campus law enforcement officers strolled an adjacent lot.

Liam meandered his way from the parking lot into the heart of the campus. Charles Winter Wood Theatre blended modestly into FAMU's historical architecture. Although he'd seen it many times before, Liam paused outside the double doors to admire the subtle bronze plaque honoring the building's namesake and pioneer of African American theater.

Inside, faint traces of fresh paint filtered the air. He slipped quietly into one of the plush red and slightly worn seats that curved around the stage in a semicircle. The wide wooden stage bore faint marks of countless productions. A complex network of lighting and sound equipment perched overhead.

Amazed as he was with the theater's modern capabilities, nothing impressed him as much as seeing Donnie in action. Liam watched his little brother offer constructive feedback to actors, demonstrating how small changes in posture or tone could elevate their performance. His ability to connect with each performer and bring out their best impressed Liam. When a prop broke, Donnie quickly came up with an alternative solution, showcasing his resourcefulness and calmness under pressure.

How did I miss this? Donnie's a natural leader. He took charge, organized the team, and paid close attention to details. All these skills translate well to managing a training program.

His phone rang. Several people on the stage, including Donnie turned in his direction. Embarrassed, Liam reached into his pocket, pulled out his phone, and silenced the noise. It was Lorraine. He mouthed an apology toward the stage and stepped outside.

"Good morning, beautiful."

"Hey, babe. Are you busy?"

"I'm at FAMU, watching one of Donnie's rehearsals."

"Aww… that's nice. I have a quick question, and I'll let you get back. Wanted to get your thoughts about food for the wedding. Would you prefer a plated dinner, buffet, or something different?"

Liam smiled. He didn't care what was served or how it was presented. All he wanted to do was marry Lorraine, but he remembered his mother's advice.

"Plated dinners, I suppose. That way, guests can relax at their tables without having to wait in line for food."

"That's right. Smart thinking. I'll let you go. Tell Donnie hello for me."

Before Liam could respond, Donnie emerged from around the corner, a scowl coated his face.

"Sure. I'll call you when I get in the office. Love you."

"Love you, too."

Liam's heart smiled. He ended the call and shoved the phone in his pocket. "Hey, little bro."

"Is everything okay? What are you doing here?" Donnie pointed a finger in his direction.

"I didn't mean to interrupt." Liam flinched. "I just wanted to watch."

"Rehearsals are closed. Why are you here? Is something wrong with Mom?"

"Mom's fine. Do you have a few minutes?"

"Sure. We have a ten-minute break. Let's take a walk."

"I've been thinking about Dad a lot lately," said Liam. "He supported both of us in his own way."

Donnie dropped his head. "Yes, he did."

"I realize now that I've been hard on you about working in the business. I blamed myself for hiring the man who embezzled money from the business."

"You didn't know. It could have happened with Dad at the reign."

"But it didn't." Liam exhaled sharply before he continued. "I started doubting myself. In part, I blamed you and Mom for not being more involved. Then Mom came to work in the office."

Donnie cocked his eyebrow. "And I worked in the field as often as I could."

"And I resented you for it. Everyone expected me to fill Dad's shoes. It was overwhelming. Being nominated for Entrepreneur of the Year made things worse."

"I understand. But the theater is where I feel most alive. It doesn't mean I don't care about the family or the business."

"I see that now. I want you to pursue your dreams, just as Dad would have wanted. And I'll be here to support you. And if it's all right with you, I'd like for you to develop a training program for our employees."

A faint smile touched Donnie's lips.

Liam knew his brother was pleased.

"You know this is a pivotal semester for me."

"I understand. You're in control. You create a project timeline, and we'll work with you."

Liam extended his hand, his fingers steady despite the weight of the moment. His lips quirked into a small grin, eyebrows raised as if to ask, *Are we good?* Donnie hesitated. His gaze dropped briefly to the floor before looking back at Liam.

Their hands connected with a solid clap, its grasp relaxing as it lingered. A slight nod exchanged between them expressed an unspoken promise to leave the friction behind. As they pulled apart, the tension between them dissolved.

Chapter 20

The University Club parking lot was a sea of headlights and brake lights, every space filled with cars, leaving latecomers circling like vultures in search of a rare, open spot.

"It looks like everyone in Tallahassee decided to attend the awards banquet," said Donnie from the driver's seat of his mother's Volvo. He pulled into the first available parking spot.

"It's like this every year." Daisy watched from the front passenger seat. "Not only is the award coveted, but the dinner is an excellent opportunity to network."

"I want to say something," announced Liam from the backseat, where he sat holding Lorraine's hand.

"What is it, dear?" asked Daisy, undoing her seatbelt. She and Donnie turned to face Liam. With only the moonlight and the parking lot lights, the car was dim.

"I appreciate your love and support throughout this entire process." Lorraine gently squeezed his hand.

Donnie smiled. "We know."

"And whether I win this award or not, I'm grateful for all of you."

"Are you gonna get all mushy on me, bro? Cause if you are, I'm outta here!"

Daisy smiled, glancing toward Lorraine. "They've been like this since they were little boys."

Lorraine shrugged. "I think it's hilarious."

Liam unbuckled his seatbelt and scooted forward. "All joking aside, I'd like to pray before we go inside."

After Liam led the foursome in prayer, they exited the car.

The parking lot buzzed with activity. The sky above, a profound shade of indigo, radiated a warm glow over the horizon. A gentle breeze rustled through the trees that lined the parking lot.

Once inside, they waited by the elevator with a group of people. Based on their formal attire, Daisy assumed everyone was headed to the third-floor Grand Ballroom for the evening's event. She gazed at her small family and smiled when she saw Lorraine's eyes trail Liam's black suit. She remembered looking at Harold that same way when he wore his formal suits to previous award galas. Liam's tuxedo jacket hugged his broad shoulders and chest before tapering slightly at the waist.

"You look nice." Lorraine stood on her tiptoes, placing a sweet kiss on Liam's cheek.

"I have to agree." Daisy's smile reached her ears.

"You look all right." Donnie teased. "But even on your best day, you can't and don't look better than me." He smoothed his palm over his face.

Giggles broke out from those within earshot.

The doors flew open. Daisy and her crew joined a few others on the elevator. The small space quickly saturated with a medley of colognes and perfumes. A whirlwind of scents, from the woody notes of cedar to the velvety scent of rose cloyed the atmosphere.

Soon, the doors opened again and ushered in a blast of fresh air. They stepped into a masterpiece of classic elegance. Crystal chandeliers hung from the vaulted ceiling, casting a warm, golden glow over the room. Rich mahogany paneling and tasteful artwork adorned the walls.

"Wow," said Lorraine, looking around the room. "I feel like I'm at the Royal Ball in the King's palace."

"The University Club is a nice place to hold an event. Have you considered this venue for your wedding reception?" asked Daisy.

"It's on my list of places to check out. But I was thinking about using the location where we held the engagement party. It was beautiful. It also has two other ballrooms. Liam said that you know the owner. Is that right?" asked Lorraine.

"Yes, I do." Daisy's thoughts pulled her back to the night of the engagement party. She knew then that something special was growing between Zeke and her. It was that night they shared their first kiss.

"Mom …" Daisy's train of thought broke at the sound of Liam's voice. A young blond girl, wearing a white blouse tucked into black trousers, stood next to him. Everyone appeared to be waiting for her.

"Follow Kasey," Liam continued. "She's going to usher us to our table."

Kasey offered a quick smile and a wave. Then she turned and began meandering through the crowded dining room. Daisy admired the table centerpieces, each with a low fresh flower arrangement surrounded by a small votive candle in a clear glass holder. Kasey and her bouncy blond ponytail stopped at the table with the number twenty-one displayed in a sleek silver frame.

"Thank you," Liam said.

Donnie gently pulled a chair out from the table for this mother and carefully pushed the chair in as she sat. Liam did the same for Lorraine.

Everyone rearranged name places so Liam and Lorraine shared a spot next to each other, forming a cozy pair. Donnie sat between Liam and Daisy. And Daisy secured the spot next to her seat for Rosie.

"You're expecting others?" asked Kasey, glancing at the remaining empty chairs.

"Yes. They should be here soon."

"Awesome. Your server will arrive with beverages shortly. Is there anything I can get you now?"

Liam glanced around the table before answering for everyone. "No. But thank you."

While the others chatted, Daisy scanned the room. She hadn't seen or spoken with Zeke in weeks. From experience, she knew all business owners in the area were invited and hoped he had accepted the invitation. She looked forward to seeing him again. Would he acknowledge her presence? Would he be happy to see her? She wasn't sure, but time would tell.

Daisy caught sight of Kasey escorting Rosie and Donzel to the table. Kasey waved her hand toward the empty chairs like she was modeling a refrigerator on "The Price is Right." Daisy stood, opening her arms for a hug. "Donzel! Rosie! It's so good to see you both."

Liam stood and delivered a firm handshake to Donzel and a quick hug to Rosie. "Thank you for coming."

"Looking good," said Donnie, shaking hands with Donzel.

"Thank you, sir. I'm just trying to keep up with you."

"And you, Ms. Rosie. You look fabulous," said Donnie before giving her a light hug.

Lorraine smiled warmly from across the table. "Hello. It's nice to see you again."

Donzel pulled out the chair next to Daisy and motioned for Rosie to sit.

"Thank you, sweetheart." Rosie gave her husband a small kiss on the cheek. Then she turned to Daisy. "Girl, I thought we'd never get here. Traffic was terrible."

"You made it. That's all that matters." Daisy's eyes darted toward the door.

"Congratulations. This is an honor. I know your father would be proud," said Donzel to Liam.

Liam placed one hand over his heart. "Thank you, sir."

The server arrived, poured water into their glasses, and disappeared.

"I saw him in the lobby," Rosie told Daisy as she leaned close to her ear.

Daisy furrowed her brows as if she didn't understand.

"Don't even try it. You know exactly who I'm talking about," Rosie tossed a don't-play-with me look with curled lips, creased brows and head slanted to one side. "And don't be so obvious. Even Stevie Wonder could see that you're looking for someone."

Daisy's heart dropped. It'd been almost one month since she'd seen him, inhaled a whiff of his woodsy scent, or felt the touch of his strong but gentle hands. Part of her wanted to rush out to find him, but she maintained her composure.

Rosie noticed Donnie watching his mother. "I was impressed with the dinner selections. I chose the roasted salmon. What about you?" asked Rosie, changing the subject.

"What? Oh, yes. I chose the roasted salmon, also." Daisy responded, offering her friend a nod of appreciation. Then she turned to Donnie. "Let me guess, you ordered the roasted chicken."

"I sure did."

"Ever since he was a little boy, he's loved chicken." Daisy's eyes circled the table, looking at no one in particular. "I could bake it, boil it, broil it, fry it, or throw it on the grill. It didn't matter, he loved yard bird."

"I can relate," agreed Donzel.

Daisy chatted along with the others discussing stocks, bonds, and local politics. Thanks to Rosie, she was able to keep her mind on the table conversation for a few minutes. That is until she noticed Kasey walking toward them followed by Zeke and his business partner.

Chapter 21

Kasey sat Arthur and Zeke at a table with two beautiful women a few rows in front of them. The men offered greetings to the ladies, who used their perfectly manicured hands to point out the nameplates. Was this a double date or had they been randomly seated at the same table? Arthur slipped into the chair next to one of the ladies and Zeke sat beside the other, positioning himself in Daisy's direct view.

Now she could spend the entire evening pretending not to notice him.

"How's the wedding planning coming along?" Rosie asked Lorraine.

"So far, so good. Things were overwhelming at first. My job requires a lot of travel, and Liam is always busy with work. We decided to hire a wedding planner. She's a tremendous help."

"Are you planning a big wedding?" asked Donzel, taking a sip of water.

"We wanted something small and intimate, but the list keeps growing," Liam glanced at his fiancé.

Rosie cleared her throat before speaking. "Want some advice from an old married lady?"

"Sure." Lorraine smiled. "I need all the help I can get."

"Keep it simple and save your money." Rosie shook her finger between the both of them.

 Donzel and Daisy nodded in agreement.

"Thank you," said Lorraine. "That's wise advice. I can see how keeping things simple could make it easier to focus on what truly matters. I'll definitely keep that in mind."

A member of the catering staff arrived, delivering fresh salads and the main course to the table. When everyone was served, Donzel blessed the food. The group continued to chat as they dined. Daisy busied herself with eating her meal. Even with slow, deliberate bites, her mind kept drifting back to Zeke. Her heart raced as she wondered if they would get a chance to speak. If so, what would she say? And how would he react to seeing her?

Conversations echoed around the table, but she was unaware of what was said or who was speaking. Zeke's presence drew her undivided attention. Couldn't he feel her presence as well? Had he forgotten her already? She had no one to blame but herself. He had a right to move on.

Then suddenly, as if on instinct, he turned in her direction. His eyes linked with hers before slowly circling the table. Daisy detected a frown as though he'd remembered the words she'd spoken to him about her sons.

Zeke gave a slight nod of acknowledgment then turned his attention to the people at his table.

Perhaps he regrets seeing me again.

"Time for dessert," Rosie said, looking at her anxiously as if she too had seen Zeke's reaction.

"They're going to announce the winners soon," said Lorraine in a soft voice, tossing her arm around Liam in an affectionate hug. "I'm too nervous to eat."

Daisy dared not look in Zeke's direction again. She pretended he wasn't there.

"Mom, please remain cool when they call out his name," said Donnie.

"Of course. I know how to behave."

Liam wiggled a finger in the air. "Like the time you yelled out at my sports banquet?"

"That was a mistake, and it doesn't count."

"What happened?" asked Lorraine.

"Do tell," said Daisy.

"I guess I was in sixth or seventh grade. My buddy won an award, and we all clapped for him. I yelled his name, Tripp. Only

Mom thought I was antagonizing him." Liam couldn't complete the story for laughing, so Donnie finished it for him.

"Mom thought Liam was telling the boy to trip and fall. She reprimanded Liam right there in the middle of everything and everybody."

Rosie turned to her friend. "Tell me you didn't embarrass your son like that."

Daisy rebuffed Rosie's words with a wave of her hand. "Like I said, it was a simple mistake. And I apologized for it."

Before long, a tall blond woman stood behind the podium and introduced herself as the host for the evening. The room was filled with a subtle upsurge of activity. Chairs scraped lightly against the polished floor, as attendees pivoted to face the speaker. After a short oration on the history of entrepreneurship, she introduced the guest speaker. As customary, the reigning Entrepreneur of the Year was given the honor. He spoke for a few minutes about his experiences. The host returned to the podium.

"Good evening, everyone. Tonight, we are here to celebrate some of Tallahassee's finest business minds, individuals who have not only excelled in their industries but have also made a significant impact on our community. We had an incredibly competitive cohort this year with five exceptional finalists who have all demonstrated extraordinary vision and leadership. While every finalist is deserving of recognition, only three can be awarded tonight. Now it's time to reveal who will be taking home the top honors.

In third place, we have a local favorite. A bakery that has sweetened our lives and given back to the community in countless ways. Please join me in congratulating Debra Lyons, owner of Debra's Den of Delights."

The air buzzed with enthusiasm as Ms. Lyons stepped forward to accept her award. Moments later, the audience held its breath, waiting for the next announcement.

"Our second-place winner is the owner of a new car dealership, who has gone above and beyond to support local initiatives while building a successful business. Please help me congratulate Douglass Broomfield, owner of Douglass Motors."

After Mr. Broomfield accepted his award and descended the stage, the room fell silent. Daisy held her breath. The wait was agonizing but riveting, every fiber of her being wanted to hear Liam's name called.

"And finally, our first-place winner, who has earned this honor through hard work and a deep commitment to community service, is the owner of Whittington Landscaping. Congratulations, Liam Whittington, on this well-deserved recognition."

Everyone at the table stood, applauding as Liam clasped his hands together in a prayer-like position. He rose from his seat, wrapped his arms around Lorraine, and placed a tender kiss on her cheek.

Wiping a tear from her eye, Lorraine whispered, "Congratulations, baby. I'm proud of you."

"Thank you," Liam responded.

Then he turned to Donnie, who yanked him into a big bear hug. The smile on Donnie's face told everyone he was happy for his brother. "Congratulations, bro. You worked hard, and you deserve it!"

Stepping to his mother, Liam pulled her in his arms and held her for a few moments. Daisy's eyes filled with tears at this noble tribute being imparted to her son. She'd seen his hard work and dedication. He deserved this.

Liam released her. "This never would have happened without you. Thank you for your support and encouragement," he whispered.

Inhaling deeply, Daisy touched her chest. Her pulse raced like a lawnmower tearing through tall grass. She watched as Liam made his way to the microphone. She felt Rosie's arm finding its way around her shoulders. Daisy appreciated the kind gesture but couldn't pull her eyes away from Liam.

Liam stood at the platform, the gleaming award in his hand captured the soft glow of the chandeliers above. The applause faded, leaving the room draped in expectant silence.

"First, I'd like to thank my Lord and Savior, Jesus Christ. He has given me a life that is bigger and better than anything I could ask or think." Raising his index finger, Liam looked to Heaven.

Daisy bowed her head. "Thank You, Jesus," she whispered.

Liam continued, "I'm deeply honored to receive this award. Whittington Landscaping is more than just a job—it's my family legacy. I want to begin by thanking my mother." Liam's eyes fell on Daisy. "You believed in me when I didn't believe in myself. You came out of retirement to guide me in the office with your wisdom and experience. Thank you, Mom."

Daisy threw a few air kisses his way.

Next, he locked eyes with Donnie. "To my brother, who has juggled his college studies while still working in our business – your support means everything to me." Liam placed his hand over his heart, nodding toward his brother.

"My father always told us that life is about moving forward, no matter how hard things get. He wanted us to be happy and to carry on his legacy, not with sadness but with joy."

Liam paused, scanned the room, then continued. His voice was steady but filled with emotion. "When my father passed, I struggled to figure out how to move on. He was the foundation of our family, our business, our dreams. But then I remembered his wish for us—to live fully and be happy, I knew the best way to honor him was to not just run the business, but to grow it, and to live my life in a way that would make him proud. This award is more than just recognition of hard work; it's proof that we can heal, move forward, and find joy again, just as my father wanted. Dad, this one's for you."

As a standing ovation filled the air with energy, Liam's speech roused something deep within Daisy. For years, she thought holding on to Harold's memory was the only way to preserve their love. But as she listened to her son talk about moving forward, she realized with surprising clarity–Harold had wanted the same for her. It wasn't Harold who held her back, but her fear of letting him go. He would have wanted her to embrace life again.

Applause thundered through the room, but slowly, the clapping began to fade, and the room settled into a calm hush. With everyone seated, Liam turned his attention to Lorraine. Time seemed to stall, his eyes filled with love and gratitude. A murmur rippled through the crowd as they followed his line of sight, but it was as if he hardly noticed. He lowered his head slightly, his voice barely audible but filled with reverence. "God is good," he murmured, the sincerity of the moment filling the room with a quiet sense of awe.

Liam blinked and cleared his throat. "To my incredible fiancée, Lorraine, you've been a constant source of strength. You inspire me every day to be the best version of myself, and I'm blessed to have you in my life. And I can't wait to make you my wife."

Lorraine placed two fingers on her lips, then motioned to send kisses in his direction.

"I want to extend my deepest gratitude for the nomination. Your belief in my work means the world to me. To the people of Tallahassee, I cannot thank you enough for your unwavering support. You've made this city not just a place to work, but a place to call home. Thank you for believing in what we've built together."

"I'm humbled and grateful to the business community for casting your votes in my favor. Knowing that my fellow entrepreneurs recognize my efforts is truly one of the greatest honors I could receive. Thank you again, and may God bless you all."

Liam returned to the table and to the people who loved him the most. After a few closing words from the host, well-wishers bombarded the table with congratulatory messages.

Although it was only nine o'clock, Daisy was exhausted from all the excitement. She needed a moment to herself. She took advantage of the break to stroll through the lobby. The crowded foyer bustled with people trying to avoid what was sure to be heavy traffic leaving the campus.

As she made her way past the elevators, Daisy saw a handful of people enjoying the view from the windows. She continued past them and headed around the corner, deciding it was far enough away to enjoy a few moments alone. Strolling a little further down the hall, she saw a couple taking advantage of the secluded area passionately embracing against the wood paneling.

She discovered an open spot near a large window offering a view of the campus.

Harold's words to 'move on and be happy' were not just for Liam and Donnie. They were for me as well. Have I missed my opportunity to move on?

All her anxious thoughts about dishonoring Harold by entering a new relationship had dissipated. She'd been so worried about preserving their love that she'd missed an opportunity to begin again. If only she could turn back time. She would tell Liam and Donnie about Zeke. What good would it do to tell them now? Zeke had obviously moved on.

"Congratulations to Liam on a job well done."

Daisy's entire body tingled when she recognized the voice resounding from beyond her shoulders.

"Hi, Zeke," she whispered.

Chapter 22

Daisy pasted on a counterfeit smile, expecting to see him standing with one of the women from his table. To her surprise, Zeke was alone. Suddenly, she couldn't find her voice. Nervousness gripped her, keeping her as still as an oak tree rooted firmly in well-drained soil.

Her heart hammered as she stood across from Zeke, the man she had chosen to walk away from. Yet, here she was, straining to keep her distance. Her hands ached to reach out, to feel the warmth of his embrace just one more time. She fought the urge with everything she had, tightening her fingers into fists at her sides as if holding on to her reserve.

A part of her longed to run into his arms and hold on forever, but Esther's words echoed in her mind: *Please, don't bring him more pain than he's already endured. He deserves happiness.*

"I can see why you're so proud of him." Zeke flashed his award-winning smile.

"Thank you," she said softly. She wanted to walk away, but her legs wouldn't cooperate.

"And, that speech … it's obvious he loves and cares for you," Zeke spoke as if nothing had changed between them. Maybe they could reconnect by rebuilding the friendship. What about the woman at his table?

Don't jump to conclusions.

"Thanks. I believe he does."

She drew in a long breath. He smelled good and looked even better than she remembered.

Zeke nodded. "I'm glad I decided to attend."

"So am I."

Just be direct. Ask him about the woman at the table.

"I should get going. I'm sure they're looking for me. Your party is probably looking for you as well," said Daisy.

She prepared herself emotionally but hoped she still had a chance.

"My party? Oh, you mean Arthur? He's probably flirting with one or both of the women we met tonight. Our seats were randomly assigned."

Daisy tried to hide her satisfaction.

Zeke placed his hands in his pants pocket. "Before you leave, there's something I need to say."

The sincerity of his words tugged at her heart.

"Yes?"

"I owe you an apology. I sent Esther to meet you at my office that day. It was painful enough saying goodbye over the phone, I didn't think I could see you and maintain my distance."

"You don't owe me anything. Esther explained everything. She told me about your wife and …"

"… and her boyfriend, the one that was driving *my* car!" His voice quivered.

Daisy sensed his pain. She moved in closer and reached for his hand. The warmth of their touch sent shivers through her spine. "I'm sorry you experienced that. You're a good man, Zeke. You deserve better."

She expected him to pull away. Instead, he stood there, holding her hand and looking into her eyes. Was he feeling what she was feeling?

Step away, Daisy. Don't inflict any more pain on him. He deserves better.

"It was a difficult time," Zeke explained. "Just wanted to come to Tallahassee, build a thriving business, and spend my spare time visiting Esther and her family."

Zeke slowly released her hand.

"Esther loves you very much. You've done a great job as a father. I could tell just from chatting with her for a few minutes, she would do anything to protect you."

"Thank you. I would do anything for her as well."

Pausing for a moment, they held each other's gaze. Her feelings were a tempest inside her, swirling between sadness and longing, with desire sparkling through the air like static. She bit her lip, trying to concentrate, but the intensity of Zeke's gaze made it difficult. Their desire to kiss was palpable, pulling them together like a magnet irresistibly drawn to iron. Every inch of her wanted to close the gap.

Daisy took a quick peep over Zeke's shoulder. Donnie, Liam, and Lorraine were headed in her direction.

"My sons–" she whispered.

Zeke hung his head and took a deep breath. "I know you need to get back. It was nice to see you again."

"I was going to say my sons are here. Would you like to meet them?"

Chapter 23

Liam and Donnie looked like angry bulls. Their eyes were intense with fury and their bodies taut as if they were ready to charge the moment they saw her chatting with a strange man. Liam seemed to relax a bit when Lorraine whispered something in his ear. Perhaps it was a reminder that Daisy was a grown woman.

Zeke pivoted, now facing the oncoming threat. Removing his hands from his pocket, he stood erect like a Marine reporting for duty. With no signs of anxiety, he appeared ready to take on what was ahead.

Liam's eyes shifted from Daisy to Zeke, then back to Daisy. The creases in his forehead deepened. Obviously, he remembered meeting Zeke at the engagement party, but he still wasn't pleased.

Small lines of confusion swept across Donnie's brow. His eyes fixed on Zeke. The corner of his mouth twitched upward, forming a silent question. He tilted his head slightly to one side.

"Mom, what's going on here?" asked Liam.

This is it! It's now or never. Declare your feelings for Zeke even if it means risking rejection.

Daisy raised her hand toward Liam as if pushing back the walls of questions and confusion.

"Everyone, this is Zeke. I wasn't ready to introduce you all before, but that was a mistake I regret. Zeke deserves better than that, and I want you to meet him because he's important to me. And if he's still interested, I'd like to spend a lot more time with him. I hope you'll give him a chance."

Liam and Donnie exchanged a puzzled look.

Zeke extended his hand toward Liam. "It's nice to see you again. Congratulations on your award."

Daisy could almost see the pieces falling into place in Liam's head as he absorbed the information. After a moment of hesitation, Liam thrust his hand for the handshake.

"It's nice to see you again, Mr. Daniel. This is my fiancé, Lorraine."

"Nice to meet you, sir." Lorraine grinned from ear to ear.

Zeke turned to introduce himself to Donnie. "And you must be the thespian. It's nice to finally meet you."

"Likewise, I look forward to getting to know more about you."

Zeke reached for Daisy's hand, and his touch was as soothing as a warm cup of coffee gripped between her hands.

"I know it's late, but we were about to head home for a small celebration. Would you like to join us?" asked Donnie.

"We were?" asked Liam, apparently surprised by his brother's announcement.

Donnie swung an arm around his brother's shoulder. "You know Mom wouldn't let this night pass without an official celebration."

Daisy looked at Zeke. "Well, what do you say? Will you join us?"

"It would be my pleasure."

Six months later

Daisy pulled into the parking lot of Elegant Events. She checked her appearance in the mirror before exiting the car. A different set of eyes looked back at her. The sad eyes that held on to memories of the past, were now replaced with eyes filled with hope for the future. She reapplied a coat of her favorite MAC Ruby red lip color and stepped out of the car.

It was as if God created the morning, especially for her. The refreshing cool morning was a welcomed break from the lingering summer heat. A gentle breeze rustled through the trees, and the beautiful blue sky set a peaceful mood. She made a mental note to enjoy a brisk walk before the day warmed up.

As she neared the front of the building, the doors opened. Zeke stepped out with a smile.

"Good morning, beautiful."

"Hi."

Before she could utter another word, Zeke moved in for a tender kiss.

A few months earlier, she would have made a mad dash for the front door before anyone could see their display of affection. Instead, she returned the gesture with little regard for who might be watching. After a series of butterfly kisses, Zeke ushered her through the door and into the ballroom.

"As you know, this is our largest room. It can accommodate everyone on the list."

"Are you sure about gifting us the use of the facility? We're more than willing and able to pay the fee."

"Consider it my wedding gift to Liam and Lorraine. It would be an honor."

"Now, I haven't seen you since yesterday. I'm going to need more than a few pecks on the lips."

He pulled her in for a passionate kiss.

"Hold that thought," he said, waving one finger in the air. "I'll be right back."

Zeke left the room in a hurry; within minutes, the atmosphere was filled with Luther Vandross crooning softly from the overhead speakers, "Never too Much." Daisy couldn't help but smile, tap her feet, and sway to the music.

Zeke returned singing the lyrics and smiling. Then he reached for Daisy, and they swayed to the music together. They lost track of time.

After the third song ended, he released her. They were surprised to see Liam and Lorraine dancing on the other side of the room.

"When did you two get here?" asked Daisy.

"A little while ago," replied Liam. "But you were too caught up to notice."

Daisy and Lorraine giggled.

"My apologies," said Zeke, his smile was all teeth. "It's just that when I'm with your mother …"

"Please!" Liam threw one hand in the air, ignoring Zeke's words like holding down the lid on a pot that was just about to boil over. "I ain't mad at 'cha. I just don't want to hear about it."

"Me neither," said Donnie walking into the room. He hugged Daisy and gave Liam a high five. Then he hugged Lorraine.

"Hands off my woman!" teased Liam.

They shared a group laugh.

Donnie shook Zeke's hand. "Seriously, it's nice to see Mom happy again."

"Trust me," said Zeke, placing his hand on his chest. "I'm the grateful one. She's shown me what happiness looks like."

Daisy paused for a moment and looked into Zekes eyes. "Honestly, I never thought I'd feel this way again. My heart was on hold for so long because it knew what it was waiting for:

something genuine, something lasting, something worth the risk. God has truly turned my mourning into dancing again."

171

Acknowledgments

First, I give all glory and honor to my heavenly Father, the author and finisher of my faith. Lord, You have placed the desire to write in my heart, and in Your faithfulness, You have guided me every step of the way. As Psalm 37:4 declares, "Delight thyself also in the Lord; and he shall give thee the desires of thine heart." Thank You for reminding me of my purpose and for using my writing to share Your love.

To Donald: thank you for encouraging me to chase my dreams and giving me the time and space to make them a reality. Your unwavering support and shared excitement over every milestone mean more to me than words can express. Thank you for being my sounding board and for sharing your own stories and experiences that have influenced my work. Your belief in me keeps me going, and I'm so grateful to have you by my side.

To Ashley and Michael: thank you for cheering me on every step of the way and celebrating every milestone with me. Your pride in my work gives me the courage to keep going, and your personality traits and stories inspire so many of the characters I create. Your excitement each time a book is published reminds me of the joy of storytelling. I couldn't do this without you!

To my wonderful readers: thank you for your incredible support, whether through buying my books, leaving thoughtful reviews, or sharing my work with others. You inspire me every day to keep writing and exploring new stories, and I'm so grateful for the time you invest in reading my words. Your encouragement fuels my creativity, and I couldn't do this without you.

To Ann Marie Bryant and the team at Victorious by Design, Denise M. Walker and the team at Armor of Hope Writing & Publishing Services, LLC: thank you for your loyalty and for refining my ideas, enhancing my voice, and catching the inconsistencies I couldn't see. Your dedication has elevated this novel in ways I couldn't have achieved alone.

To Barbara Joe Williams and Amani Publishing: your impeccable attention to detail and unwavering professionalism have made this manuscript shine. I am so grateful for your dedication to ensuring every word was just right.

To Margo Thomas, thank you for you encouragement, wisdom, and careful reading. You are a treasure.

To my mentor, Brian W. Smith: thank you for your invaluable guidance, which helped shape the structure of *Hearts on Hold*. Your mentorship not only boosted my confidence but also taught me to work with the end in mind. I will carry these lessons with me in every story I write.

About the Author

W. Mason Dunn is a best-selling author and accomplished writing consultant who is passionate about spreading the Gospel through her literary works. She has written and published six novels with many more in development.

Born in Bossier City, Louisiana, W. Mason Dunn values continuous learning and self-improvement. She earned an undergraduate degree in Business Administration from Texas College and a graduate degree in Public Administration from the University of Oklahoma.

With over two decades of experience as a higher education counselor for the military, she gained invaluable insights while traveling extensively with her husband during his 20 years of distinguished service in the United States Marine Corps. These personal and professional experiences have deeply influenced her storytelling.

W. Mason Dunn is a devoted wife of nearly four decades to her husband, Donald, and the proud mother of two adult children, Ashley and Michael Dunn. When she is not working on her next literary project, she enjoys reading, playing Scrabble, solving crossword puzzles, and helping others.

Other Books by W Mason Dunn

More Than Sisters

Faithful Father Synopsis

A Family Dilemma Synopsis

Positions Of Compromise

For Such A Time As This

Keeping Receipts

Discussion Questions

1. Daisy struggled with the fear that loving again might dishonor her late husband. Have you ever faced a situation where moving forward felt like letting go of something or someone important? How did you navigate it?

2. The story highlights love after loss. How do you think love changes or evolves after experiencing grief?

3. Liam feels undeserving of recognition for his hard work. Have you ever struggled with imposter syndrome or doubted your accomplishments? How did you overcome those feelings?

4. Family dynamics played a big role in the story. How has your family shaped your views on responsibility, forgiveness, or love?

5. Daisy believed her relationship with Harold was a part of who she was. How do past relationships—romantic or otherwise—shape our identity, even after they end?

6. Liam and Donnie's tension reflected the challenges of balancing family responsibilities. Have you ever felt overwhelmed by expectations within your family? How do you communicate your needs in those situations?

7. The love between Daisy and her sons was a central theme. What are some ways we can express unconditional love to the people closest to us?

8. The story reflected God's love for His people. How do you experience or recognize God's love in your daily life?

9. Daisy's journey involved trusting that it was okay to embrace new beginnings. What's a new beginning in your life that requires courage and faith?

10. The theme of second chances runs throughout the story. Is there a time when you were given a second chance or gave one to someone else? How did it change you?

Great stories are even better when they're shared. If Hearts on Hold touched you, here are a few simple ways to help it find its next reader:

1. Leave a review on Amazon. It only takes a minute, but it makes a world of difference.

2. Snap a pic and share it on social media. Tell folks what you loved most—whether it was a character, a moment, or just the way it made you feel.

3. Pass it on. Send a note to a friend who'd enjoy it too—or better yet, surprise them with a copy.

Thanks so much for reading. I'm so glad you spent time with this story.